He scowled at her, and Annika laughed.

She laughed and she kept right on laughing. The lights were too bright, and she was too pretty, and his body pulsed as if he'd been some kind of monk—possibly for years—and then he was moving.

Without thought, when he never acted without thinking it through.

Never—but then he was reaching down and wrapping his hands around the tops of her arms.

And then he thought a lot about the way she stopped laughing, her green eyes going wide, and that sensual mouth of hers dropping open. Especially when she made the sweetest little sound.

Ranieri lifted her up, letting the throw fall aside and the book she'd been reading crash to the floor.

He hauled her up and then, as if he'd been longing to do nothing else for the whole of his existence, Ranieri—who had never been carried away by passion in his life—slammed his mouth to Annika's at last.

And drank her in, deep.

USA TODAY bestselling, RITA® Award–nominated and critically acclaimed author **Caitlin Crews** has written more than one hundred books and counting. She has a master's and PhD in English literature, thinks everyone should read more category romance and is always available to discuss her beloved alpha heroes. Just ask. She lives in the Pacific Northwest with her comic book artist husband, is always planning her next trip and will never, ever, read all the books in her to-be-read pile. Thank goodness.

Books by Caitlin Crews

Harlequin Presents

The Sicilian's Forgotten Wife
The Bride He Stole for Christmas

Pregnant Princesses

The Scandal That Made Her His Queen

Rich, Ruthless & Greek

The Secret That Can't Be Hidden
Her Deal with the Greek Devil

The Lost Princess Scandal

Crowning His Lost Princess
Reclaiming His Ruined Princess

Visit the Author Profile page
at Harlequin.com for more titles.

Caitlin Crews

—

WILLED TO WED HIM

HARLEQUIN
PRESENTS

HARLEQUIN®
PRESENTS™

ISBN-13: 978-1-335-73865-3

Willed to Wed Him

Copyright © 2022 by Caitlin Crews

For questions and comments about the quality of this book, please contact us at CustomerService@Harlequin.com.

Harlequin Enterprises ULC
22 Adelaide St. West, 41st Floor
Toronto, Ontario M5H 4E3, Canada
www.Harlequin.com

Printed in U.S.A.

Recycling programs for this product may not exist in your area.

WILLED TO WED HIM

This one is for Flo, who I will be lost without!

CHAPTER ONE

ANNIKA SCHUYLER STARED across the disturbingly overpolished conference room table in disbelief.

"THAT'S IMPOSSIBLE," she said.

Not for the first time. Possibly not even for the tenth time, which would have embarrassed her if she wasn't so *beside herself.*

"Your father made his wishes excruciatingly clear," said the head lawyer, Stanley Something-or-other, who distinguished himself from the crowd of them who cluttered up the whole of the opposite side of the table by managing to look sorrowful. As if this turn of events had taken him, personally, by surprise.

Judging by the avid, too-shrewd expressions on all the other faces staring back at her, Annika suspected that she was the only one who was actually shocked.

"His wishes might be clear," she managed to say, "but I'm pretty sure they're not actually *legal*."

Annika tried to settle herself, but panic and something a lot like desperation clawed at her as she sat there at the long table. Everyone else in the nosebleed-high law firm conference room, some fifty floors up from the New York streets, looked cool and corporate. The way she'd planned to look herself, because she'd expected the reading of her father's will today to be tough. It didn't matter that Bennett Schuyler, IV, had been effectively lost years before his death at the start of the month. He had still been here and now he wasn't.

She had expected this to be painful for emotional reasons. And it was, but she couldn't stop obsessing about the fact that in a room full of calmly suited white-collar warriors, she was nothing but disheveled. She could see her own reflection in the shiny tabletop and there was no getting around it. She'd thought it would be lovely—read: soothing, and Annika needed some of that these days—to walk down into midtown Manhattan from the Upper East Side for this meeting. Alas, she had overestimated the comfort of her *cool and corporate* shoes.

That situation had spiraled quickly. And so, now, her hair was disastrous, she'd had to come hobbling into the meeting while everyone else had been about *masterful strides*, and she was not entirely sure that her deodorant was up to the task of the overly hot September day outside, the shock of her father's will, and, of course, *him*.

Ranieri Furlan, who currently stood with his back to the room, hands clasped behind him, looking out at the city splayed out at his feet in the last of the summer sunshine.

He, naturally, looked as if men's fashion had been developed purely to celebrate his astonishing physique and that intensity of his that made grown men go doe-eyed when he walked in the room. To say nothing of what it did to weak-willed women.

If there was a more irritating man alive, Annika had yet to meet him. She had no desire to meet him.

She'd expected today to be her emancipation from this man. Not...

God, she couldn't even *think* it.

"Your father has not insisted that you behave in any particular way," Stanley, or maybe it was Stuart, was telling her. "That would certainly be legally questionable. Let me be clear. You can walk out of here today wholly unencumbered by your father's wishes in regard to one small fraction of his estate, as the rest will pass to you. All he has done is lay out a set of conditions regarding two specific parts of his estate and certain consequences that will accrue if particular benchmarks are not reached. If, within three months of the reading of this will, an

independent review by this law firm finds that you
are not married, Schuyler House will be donated to
the city. If, in those three months, Mr. Furlan is not
married, he will forfeit his position as CEO of the
Schuyler Corporation. If you are not married to each
other, there will be significant penalties. You will
be barred from working at Schuyler House entirely.
Mr. Furlan will be officially censured."

Annika had really hoped that she'd gone a little
hysterical and had imagined the breadth and depth
of the hole her father had left her in—but she had
not. Her father wanted her married or he would take
away Schuyler House, the museum Annika's grandparents had made from the home that had been built
for her Gilded Age ancestors. It was quirky and
beautiful and filled with art and antiquities, and
Annika had loved it since she was a child. She had
gotten an Art History degree at Wellesley for the
express purpose of dedicating her life to her family's tangible, accessible legacy, right there on the
Upper East Side in the original Schuyler family
home. It was the next best thing to actually having
family, she'd often thought.

She was the last Schuyler. The museum helped
her feel less alone, surrounded by so much of her
family over the ages. Their things. Their treasures.
Their portraits. The museum connected her to all
of them.

That was the part that had made her lapse off into a little bit of private hysteria. Now, as she forced herself to really pay attention this time, she realized it was much worse.

There was a fine if she was not engaged within twenty-four hours of the reading of the will. There was a fine if she was not engaged to Ranieri. There was a fine if she did not share a home with Ranieri, or whoever she was engaged to, within a week. She was not only to be married within the month, but significant financial penalties—to be taken out of the money her father had left her—applied if she did not remain married for at least a year. If she achieved any or all of these things, yet was to blame for any of them failing—whether she called off an engagement, initiated a divorce, or refused to marry—she would lose Schuyler House. She supposed it was meant to be some small comfort that if Ranieri—or, presumably, whatever other fool she could coerce into proposing to her in the next twenty-four hours, an unlikely endeavor given she wasn't dating anyone and hadn't in ages—faced his own set of financial penalties, to be taken out of his compensation package.

Though, of course, the penalties if the groom in question *wasn't* Ranieri were less about taking things away and more about what he wouldn't be getting. No bonuses, no stock options, no bribes at all.

Thanks a lot, Dad, Annika thought darkly.

"Do you understand?" asked Stephen, or whatever he was called. And this time, she did not find the kindly look on his face at all encouraging.

"I understood the first time," Annika assured him. She attempted a smile, but didn't quite pull it off. "Until today I was under the impression my father loved me."

She realized when she said it that the army of lawyers now all thought she was terribly sad. When what she was actually struggling to keep inside was her temper.

Really, Dad, she thought then. *What were you thinking?*

Annika wasn't looking at him directly and yet still she was aware that this was the moment Ranieri decided to move. He turned back around to face the long conference room, and Annika was certainly not the only one who cringed away from the ferocity he wore as easily as that dark suit, exquisitely tailored to simply *exult* in the lean, fine lines of his powerful body.

Ranieri Furlan came from ancient Italian stock, descended from generations upon generations of northern Italians with the same dark hair, golden eyes, and height. He was out of context here, but *there*, he would be unremarkable. Or so she liked to tell herself. She'd visited Milan once or twice and she'd assured herself for years that if they were strolling around the Duomo, she would lose him in a crowd. Ranieri would simply blend. He'd be mundane and run-of-the-mill over there.

Sadly, Annika knew that wasn't true, no matter how many times she tried to convince herself otherwise. She'd wandered the whole of the north of Italy without ever clapping eyes on a man who seemed to *simmer* like Ranieri did. Somehow, he managed to *seethe* just under the surface while remaining effortlessly sophisticated all the while.

She had no idea how he did it.

He had come to the Schuyler Corporation after doing a business degree in London and then a master's at Harvard. She had been in high school when he had so impressed her father, who had been wanting to step down from his CEO duties for some time. Ranieri had been not only driven and focused, as all those who wanted a CEO position were— he had wanted to keep the family feel of the company intact. He had believed, right from the start, that the family beginnings of Schuyler Corporation were what made it uniquely positioned to succeed in a world overrun with corporations that tended toward soullessness.

He had been speaking Bennett's love language.

Teenage Annika had not been impressed with the interloper into her family's affairs, but then, her father had not offered her a vote. And in the fullness of time, even Annika could grudgingly admit that under Ranieri, the Schuyler Corporation had bloomed. He had delivered higher profits every single year since he'd started, showed no sign of slowing down, and still maintained the core values that her father had believed in so deeply.

She knew that the financial papers swooned over him. But the papers were neck and neck with all the single women in Manhattan, if not the world, who became giddy at the very mention of his name. Annika had served as her father's hostess for years after her mother died, and had also served as his date for all the endless rounds of annual New York social events, where she had gotten to watch Ranieri's effect on the average Manhattan socialite up close.

Really, she'd made a study of him.

He was beautiful, there was no denying it, but there were a lot of beautiful men in New York City. A lot of sophisticated men, too. Ranieri was different because he had that edge. There was something about the way his features came together. The dark hair, cut brutally short, as if he wanted the intense gold of his eyes to take over rooms as he entered. As if it was deliberate. She believed it was.

Ranieri knew exactly what effect he had, and used it ruthlessly. His bold nose and stark, sensual mouth were enough to make anyone's belly flutter. His dark brows were always *about* to scowl or lift into a mocking arch. He was not given much to smiling. Or laughing, unless it was a short bark of laughter, designed to intimidate. Nor did he trouble himself to make any attempt to engage in anything that could possibly be confused for small talk.

And yet, when he felt like it, he could be charming. In his intense, urbane manner, focusing all of his considerable attention on the unwary person before him and making them *flutter*.

In a city filled with the glittery and the glamorous, Ranieri was a fierce and elegant blade—never polished enough to take away from the fact that he could kill. And easily.

He just never seemed *civilized*, was the thing.

And today it was even worse than usual.

It had been a rough five years. Her father's car accident that winter had taken everyone by surprise, perhaps Annika and Ranieri most of all. At first, everyone had imagined that Bennett Schuyler would snap back quickly. Or quickly enough. He had issued his usual commands from his hospital bed and they'd followed them, never imagining that he would slip into a coma a week after his accident.

And then linger, somewhere between death and life, for years.

Annika had imagined that the makeshift guardianship her father had insisted upon would end with his death. That Ranieri would have nothing more to do with her life, thank you very much. She was just glad that she had already graduated from college at the time of her father's accident. She wasn't so young that she would have been truly under Ranieri's thumb, and so he hadn't controlled her as much as he could have. He'd simply controlled all the money. And had taken it upon himself to act as the unwanted director of the museum, too.

You don't know what my father's wishes were for the museum, she had argued, for years.

Neither do you, Ranieri had replied in his usual obdurate fashion.

Annika had been so certain that once the will was read, she would be well shot of the man. This was not supposed to be happening.

Ranieri surveyed the room, which had fallen silent before him, as ever.

"Leave us, please," was all he said.

He didn't have to be loud. He rarely was. He simply spoke, his voice deep and rich with hints of Italy and England alike, making him sound even more intense.

The entire legal team had left the room before

Annika could even process the command. And then it was just the two of them.

Ranieri gazed at her then, and the look on his face was at least familiar. It was that rather frozen look he always aimed her way, as if he couldn't quite believe that the creature he saw before him was truly the daughter of Bennett Schuyler, renowned the world over for his business acumen and social grace. Ranieri struggled with Annika's lack of either.

She knew this because he told her so, and she could see he planned to beat that dead horse a little more today, too. *Terrific.*

"You look a mess," he told her darkly, and he was correct, of course. But why did he have to *say it*? "This is how you choose to honor your father?"

"My father actually did love me." She often tried to sound as ferocious as he did, but she could never pull it off. She was always too chirpy. That was what he had called it once. Her *incessant chirping.* "He never held me up to unrealistic standards."

"Are the standards unrealistic?" His voice cut straight through her, as ever. Ranieri was worse than a cold winter wind howling down one of the New York streets. "I passed any number of women on my way into this conference room, all of whom were apparently capable of brushing their hair."

Annika glanced at her reflection in the table

again and could manage little more than a rueful laugh. "I did brush my hair. Thank you for asking after my morning routine. It's just that I didn't brush it *again* after walking all the way here. I would have. I meant to. It's only that I had some shoe issues, and that made me late, and I thought you might have an aneurysm if I was seriously tardy. So really, if you want to blame someone, blame yourself."

He did that thing with his jaw that somehow made her think only of great stones, like monoliths set in lonely fields. "And yet you were, in fact, tardy."

Annika waved her hand. "Five minutes doesn't count."

"Try ten."

"You can take that long waiting for an elevator in a building like this." She shrugged. "And anyway, I don't really think the state of my hair is the issue here."

There were a great many issues, but she chose at that moment to concentrate on one of the major ones. That being his deep and historic dislike of her.

When she'd been younger, she'd thought that she was imagining things. She'd met the man when she was sixteen. And sure, she'd watched him be his own brand of brashly charming to everyone he met, except her. But she had been so awkward. So overset by the things her friends found so easy. What to wear, how to act, how to behave as if they were at least ten years older than they were. Her mother would have helped her with these things, she was sure, but she had died when Annika was small. Annika sometimes worried she remembered only the idea of her, handed down by those with real memories. And she felt lucky if she got her dress on the right way.

The effortlessly collected Ranieri had always looked at her as if she was the human, teenage version of a tornado. As if he fully expected her to take down the foundations of any building they sat in if she wasn't carefully watched.

As she'd gotten older, his dislike had only grown. He had made it abundantly clear that she was an embarrassment to the Schuyler name. She knew his argument. That he and her father were engaged in building that name, yet there Annika was, whirling about in her usual fashion, spreading embarrassment and chaos wherever she went. She was always too messy, too inappropriately dressed, too scatterbrained, too clumsy, too awkward.

Annika had, previous to Ranieri, considered that her own brand of charm. Her father had always smiled fondly and told her that her mother had been a tornado too—but he'd always said that like it was a good thing.

She wasn't actually used to people disliking her. Maybe everyone she encountered didn't *love* her, but they usually didn't dislike her. She wasn't the kind of woman who inspired strong feelings in others. She'd accepted that.

Only Ranieri made it clear that he not only didn't like her—she was an affront to his sensibilities in every way. Only this man, of all people.

The good news was that it didn't hurt her feelings anymore.

"I want Schuyler House and I assume you want to continue doing your CEO thing." She aimed a polite smile his way, because it was that or sob in horror. He would consider it a weakness, so that was out. "So what do you think? Elope?"

He studied her as if she'd suggested something tawdry. And she couldn't say she cared for the fluttery sensation that overtook her the moment she thought about tawdry things involving Ranieri Furlan. She couldn't say she liked it at all.

"Elope?" he asked, as if he was unfamiliar with the word.

Like most things, once Annika had the idea in her head, she could do nothing at all but roll with it. "It's a perfect solution," she told him gaily.

He was still looming there at the bottom of the table, which she figured was probably some kind of power game. If she was feeling charitable, she might say that Ranieri didn't *try* to play power games. Probably. He simply was that powerful.

But she didn't have to attempt to compete on that level. She swiveled her chair around, and lounged back in it, gazing at him like she was some kind of fat cat herself. So replete with her own majesty that she didn't need to stand and face him.

"I'm not sure why my father thought that match-making was a good use of the little time he had left," she continued. "But I think it's perfectly easy to obey the letter of the law without inconveniencing ourselves too much. We can elope easily enough. And that will instantly sort all the rest of it out. As far as living under one roof goes, that's easily done. I know you have that loft downtown. There's also the family brownstone. I'm sure both are spacious enough to allow us to live our own lives. After a year, we go our separate ways. Everyone wins."

She gazed down the table, smiling winningly.

Ranieri appeared unmoved.

Ranieri always appeared unmoved. He was a one-man Stonehenge, only less approachable.

"And how do you think this plan of yours will look?" He asked the question as if he was interrogating her. In a court of law. In which she was a known murderer or something equally distasteful. "To the casual observer?"

She stared back at him, not comprehending either the tone or his actual words. "What does it matter?"

His lips thinned. "Naturally it doesn't matter to *you*. This does not surprise me. But I have a reputation to uphold, Annika. I cannot simply hurtle about through life, heedless of the way my actions reflect on the Schuyler Corporation."

He paused, likely so she could marinate in the fact that really, he was calling her heedless. And hurtling.

But she didn't react, because what was the point when it was always the same litany from him, so he carried on. "Having to jump through hoops like these to secure a position I have already earned is insulting." That cold gold gaze of his was a slap. "It is distasteful in the extreme to imagine colleagues and rivals alike tittering over your father's stipulations. Am I ever to be taken seriously again?"

Annika had always found him about as serious as a heart attack, but refrained from saying so. "We don't have to tell anyone that these are the terms of his will if you don't want to. I don't care what anyone thinks about me."

"That is quite apparent."

She was used to his putdowns, but this one made her ears singe just that little bit. Still, she kept herself from retorting. She knew from experience that any show of temper from her produced amazement on his part that she, as ever, was so *emotional*.

"But that creates another quandary," Ranieri mused, his gaze glittering. He seemed to take pleasure in looking at her, all the way down the length of his nose as well as the table, as if going out of his way to point out to her how much better he thought he was. If this was the sort of energy he brought to his business meetings, Annika wasn't surprised that, as far she could tell, any C-suite he glanced at flung itself at his feet *en masse*. "It is entirely believable that you might wish to marry me."

"Only if you've never met me," Annika retorted, more stung by that than she really wanted to investigate.

And anyway, he was ignoring her. "No one will have any trouble believing that you have spent your life pining away for me," he said, and the truly outrageous part was that he wasn't waiting for her response. He didn't even seem to notice her outrage. He truly believed what he was saying. She would have leaped to her feet and argued the point, because how dare he, but he skewered her with another cold glare. "But I'm afraid, Annika, that it will be impossible for anyone to believe that I would ever marry you."

And then he laughed, as if the very idea was so absurd it was funny.

Annika opened her mouth to suggest he take a flying leap out the window behind him and concentrate on forgetting about her and anything having to do with her on the way down, but shut it again, hard.

Because she'd almost forgotten what happened if he goaded her into washing her hands of this.

But she doubted very much that he had. He was a master manipulator. It was literally his job.

"Don't be silly," she said instead. "Sure, your dating history is basically a Who's Who of Fashion Week, but no one will be surprised if a man who dates supermodels exclusively ends up with a normal woman. Men like you are forever settling down with unflashy women. It's how your type signals that you're taking your marriage seriously. A time-honored rite of passage for a certain kind of tragically shallow man."

"Come now, Annika." Ranieri did something with his chin that swept over her, head to toe. "You must be realistic. It is not that you're plain. It is that I am me." He shook his head as if he shouldn't have to explain this to her. "I am a man of exacting tastes. Who will ever believe, for even a moment, that I would willingly shackle myself to a woman who takes such little care with her own appearance? Who would accept that I might sport such an unsightly disaster upon my arm?"

It took her a moment to realize that the true insult here was not that he was saying these things. But that he clearly did not even register them as insults. To him, they were simply facts, not opinions.

Annika found herself gaping at him, openmouthed. Normally he would raise his dark brows and ask her if her motor skills were impaired, but today he didn't even notice.

"It is too implausible," Ranieri continued as if he was alone. Then again, *he* probably thought he always was. "Unless we wish the entire world to think that I'm conducting my own personal charity, or suffering from a head injury, we must come up with a different reason for this."

It required all the willpower Annika had to simply sit there, close her mouth, and somehow keep herself from telling this man exactly where he could go.

"Don't be too hasty, Ranieri," she cautioned him. She made herself smile, lazily, as if this was her idea of entertainment. "The head injury can always be arranged."

CHAPTER TWO

THE INSULT OF this situation ate at him.

The indignity of it all.

He almost felt as if he'd already suffered that head injury.

"Are you threatening me?" he asked. Very mildly, because even if she was, he could not conceive of a threat with less weight. "Do you plan to hurl one of your precious statues at me?"

Annika sniffed in a dismissive manner no other being alive would dare to display in his presence. "I would hardly risk damaging a Rodin on your hard head, Ranieri."

As usual, it took only moments in her company to feel the beginnings of a headache. She didn't need to use whatever statuary she had to hand. She simply existed and was irritant enough.

Ranieri could not blame Bennett Schuyler, a man he had grown to admire deeply over the years, for these machinations on behalf of his daughter. In fact, Ranieri had long wondered what was to be done about the problem of Annika, the last of the great Schuyler family. She was obviously a problem without any clear solution. New York was heaving with heiresses, but in Ranieri's experience, all of them were more or less the same.

Annika was most emphatically not the same, despite having attended the same schools and the same debutante balls. She had always stayed entirely *herself.* He had known the girl for how many years now? And in all that time, she had never managed to acquire the faintest bit of polish. Not even by accident.

Today she sat here on this most solemn occasion looking as if she'd come to the meeting via a wind tunnel. She'd arrived late and flustered. She'd come limping in, looking disheveled. Her cheeks were still unduly flushed and her dark hair was twisted up on the top of her head, but not well. Some of it was standing out as if making a break for the ceiling even as half of it fell down.

For a long time, he'd believed she *tried* to look like this. That this committed untidiness in all things was no accident, but a campaign. He had assumed this was some kind of game she played with her father, or something she did *at* him, attempting to get revenge on him for some or other manufactured teenage reason. The way he was told American teenagers often did, especially in her class.

In the years since Bennett's accident, Ranieri had come to understand, however reluctantly, that this was no act. This was the real Annika Schuyler. She was constitutionally incapable of pulling herself together. Ranieri had been forced to conclude that despite a hefty and generous personal trust, a world-class education, and the fact that she lived in one of the most fashionable cities on the planet, Annika would simply always look like this. Her dark brown hair was always in some state of disarray. Whatever clothing she wore, no matter the occasion, it was always unequal to the task set before it. He had seen her in casualwear as well as in formal attire, and it was always the same. He had come upon her in that museum of hers when she could not have been expecting to see anyone, and it was the same. It was always the same. No matter what she did, she always looked as if she'd only moments before rolled out of bed.

He told himself that the familiar sensation that swept through him at that thought was distaste. That was all.

"This all sounds like a terrible quandary for you," she said sweetly now. Too sweetly from a woman who usually spent her time scowling at him.

Openly. "Shall we call all the lawyers in and say you've defaulted before we even start?"

Ranieri decided his head would not ache. Not even in the face of such provocation. "I think not. The Schuyler Corporation is not merely an eccentric personal project, like your museum of curiosities. Many people will suffer if I am forced to abandon it."

"Schuyler House is consistently ranked as one of the city's favorite museums, *actually*," she replied, sounding offended at the notion that her stake in this was…exactly what it was. Her odd little obsession. Not quite the same thing as a major multinational concern. "Probably because its curiosities include the odd Vermeer or two mixed in with Great-Grandmother Schuyler's childhood dolls."

"I am more familiar with the museum's exhibits than I could ever wish to be after these last five years," Ranieri growled before he thought better of it, because he knew by now that engaging with Annika was a recipe for frustration. She was the most maddening woman he had ever encountered. "Not that it matters. We have to come at this issue before us in a different way."

When he said such things in the office, battalions of underlings frothed about in a frenzied attempt to impress him with their "out of the box" thinking.

Annika, by contrast, was lounging back in her

chair, looking more than a little ornery. And the real problem here was that Ranieri truly could not believe that this was happening to him.

To *him*.

He had distinguished himself by not merely wanting the best, as so many did, but having it. Always. He chose the women who graced his arm no less carefully than he chose the cars he drove. Both were picked for their fine lines and stellar performance. And the deep, rich envy they caused in anyone who looked at them.

Annika was...not in his usual categories.

So, yes, he might have understood, on some level, why Bennett Schuyler had felt he had no choice but this. How else was the old man planning to see his daughter cared for? But Ranieri was not at all certain that he could lower his standards like this. No matter what was at stake.

Don't cut off your nose to spite your face, he warned himself.

He knew full well that excessive pride had been tripping up members of his family for generations. Then again, his preferred way to deal with the ruinous Furlan pride was to create a life that supported whatever level of pride he brought to bear. His father had been stymied by the fact that while he talked a big game and could play the part, at the end of the day, he had no head for business. His grandfather, too, had been known far and wide as a too-proud man in all the worst ways—to his own detriment. Ranieri had inherited all of that.

But he had also built himself an empire.

It was not arrogance to think himself one of the most powerful men alive. It was a fact.

Ranieri preferred facts.

And now, at last, there was no other possible rival for his position. Now that Bennett Schuyler had actually died, the Schuyler Corporation was Ranieri's at last.

The penalties would be paltry to a man of his means, but still. He didn't have it in him to let it go.

Especially not because of this gray area that he'd been mired in for the past few years. Given the appearance of control but no actual control over the one remaining Schuyler family member who could challenge him, if she wished.

If, that was, she also underwent a major sea change he thought was unlikely and became the sort of serous person who could impress shareholders. Serious people did not appear at will-readings without managing to brush their hair.

He eyed Annika now. "There is only one possible reason anyone would ever believe the two of us together," he told her. When she gazed back at him blankly—insultingly blankly, in fact—he found his mouth curving. Because he knew she wouldn't like what he was about to say and he could admit he took a certain pleasure in that. "Passion."

"I beg your... *What?*"

He was not precisely *insulted* that she looked so horrified. Still, it was a further indignity. Ranieri would have to add it to the ever-growing pile.

"Sex is the only thing on this earth that would convince a man to overlook his scruples, his own long-held preferences, his reputation, and his position." He sighed, perhaps a bit more dramatically than necessary. "Though it is still quite a stretch in this case, I grant you."

"Sex," she repeated, as if he'd said a terrible curse word. "I can only assume that you are kidding."

"It explains all of this chaos," he said, warming to the subject. "Why else all this haste and hurry? If we are to be married within the month, it will cause all kinds of comment. I will let it be known that having waited respectfully these last five years in the fervent hope that your father might rouse himself from his coma, now that he is dead we can wait no longer." Ranieri was already planning out how he would launch this unlikely relationship on the world. Trying to imagine the angles, the explanations, and even the possible advantages. "It's not an elegant solution, perhaps, but I feel it will work. It gets the job done, in any case."

She stared at him in that particular way only she had. Or only she dared. Ranieri was used to vast female awe bordering on worship. He was fully aware of his effect on women.

But Annika had always been different. Always and ever *herself*. She had always looked at him as if he had just crawled out from underneath the nearest rock, and she alone could see the dirt and mud still clinging to him. It made him want to look down to see if he could see it on himself, when he knew better.

He was a Furlan. He could trace his family back to ninth-century Venice. That he recognized any American as possessing any sort of pedigree was an indulgence of the highest order.

In these recent years, when he'd had more exposure to her than before, her insolence had been worse. Or he'd been more aware of it, perhaps. It wasn't just that she looked as if she saw that mud on him. She was also notably suspicious. She always frowned at him as if she alone could see the terrible truth about him.

Until he was tempted to wonder what, in fact, that truth was. If maybe she knew something he didn't. When that was doubtful in the extreme.

Ranieri was not used to being uncomfortable. He did not appreciate that Annika alone could make him feel that way.

It was safe to say he did not appreciate Annika Schuyler at all.

But if he needed to marry her to secure, at last, what he knew he fully deserved, well. He was prepared to do that.

Even if it meant contorting himself to appear as if he might actually have found himself besotted with this creature. No matter how bizarre and out of character that seemed.

He had moved with his usual swiftness into an acceptance of what needed to happen. It only distantly occurred to him that she had not agreed to his plan.

"I just don't think that anyone will believe that or anything like that," she said now, looking at him as if he'd lapsed off into incoherence. Or as if she'd actually succeeded in providing him with that handy head injury. She looked as if she couldn't imagine any other reason he would even suggest such an absurd plan. "On any level."

"We don't really require acceptance, of course." Ranieri said that as if she'd mounted a coherent argument instead of staring at him as if he'd lost the plot. "There needs to be a rationale that people can whisper amongst themselves. They don't have to believe it so much as accept that it could exist, and then do as they normally do and gossip shamelessly about it."

He waited for her to offer the usual accolades and acceptance that his statements usually provoked in those around him. *Thank you, Ranieri, you are quite right,* she ought to say.

But this was Annika Schuyler. The only woman he had ever met who looked at him as if *he* did not make sense.

She had looked at him the same way when she was only a girl. It had only gotten worse over time.

Today she had the unmitigated gall to sit there, her hair all askew, and regard him as if he was a raving madman while she was a bastion of calm rationality.

When he could see that she had kicked off her shoes and was currently sitting in one of the most august and revered law firms in the world—priced accordingly in fifteen-minute increments—in her bare feet.

Yet her expression suggested that *he* should be embarrassed.

She wrinkled up her nose in distaste. *Distaste.* "I'm not sure that I'm interested in claiming that I'm suddenly swept away by passion for you, of all people. So suddenly and uncharacteristically swept away, in fact, that I'm suddenly flinging myself headlong into a very public marriage with the kind of man I would never, ever consider. No one who's ever met me will believe for one moment that

I could possibly end up with such a man. Not one. They are far more likely to believe that I have been blackmailed into it for nefarious purposes."

It took him long moments to accept that she had actually managed to prick his temper. He normally kept it so far under wraps that he barely thought about it any longer. And yet here, beneath the baleful gaze of a messy, impertinent girl who should have been prostrate on the floor in the face of her good fortune, he could feel it surge.

He had to stand there and fight it down, like the boy he had not been in a lifetime.

And accept that while he did so, there was a part of him that thought that if she was so heedless of the dragon she poked at, perhaps she should meet him in all his glory—

But no. He chose to be civil. He alone would choose if that should end. He would not be goaded into it by a woman who, he needed to recollect, had a vested interest in making him walk away from this and leave her to it. She wanted her silly museum. It was possible she wanted the whole company, too. He would not consider her a candidate for even a low-level corporate position, but the company did bear her name. Maybe this was all another part and parcel of her sentimentality.

In any case, whatever her motivations, he did not intend to succumb to her needling, like a child might.

Ranieri comprehended in that moment that he had almost—*almost*—committed the cardinal sin of any negotiation. He had almost underestimated his opponent.

Maybe Annika Schuyler was, at heart, the disaster she appeared to be. But that didn't mean that was *all* she was. He was grateful he'd caught himself before he'd allowed her to take advantage of the five years he'd spent attempting to be careful with her. For her father's sake.

"I understand that I am not to everyone's taste." He managed to sound almost smooth. A triumph, given the growing storm in him. "Rich, devastatingly attractive, and sought after by all and sundry can be off-putting to some, I am sure. I suppose that if left to your own devices you would be far more interested in a poor, weak man who was an assault upon the eyes?"

"I don't know," she said, tilting her head, her green eyes blazing. He didn't know why he'd never noticed that her eyes were *green* before. Not hazel. Not muddy. Pure, bright *green*. "Is the poor ugly weakling arrogant? Full of himself? Suffering from delusions of grandeur?"

"My grandeur is a fact," Ranieri replied with soft menace. "Not a delusion. As I think you are well aware."

"If you say so." Annika sniffed. "Again, this is

all a little too icky, thank you. I don't really care if the whole world knows that I was forced to marry you to retain my birthright. It doesn't make *me* look bad."

"I see." He regarded her for a long moment, and took pleasure in the way her cheeks heated. Because he liked making her uncomfortable in turn, he assured himself. That was all. "Are you throwing in the towel, then?"

"Not at all. I'm just…not agreeing to your modifications."

"But you already agreed." He shook his head slightly, as if he despaired of her. "Is this what your word is worth, Annika? No wonder your life is so… hapless. A person's word is their bond."

"Nice try."

Annika stood up then, with no apparent grace. The dress she was wearing, a perfectly serviceable linen sheath, was a wrinkled mess. Her hair had slid farther down the back of her head, so she looked truly bedraggled. And she winced as she stood, reminding him that she, apparently, didn't know how to walk in her shoes. Even when she wasn't wearing them.

She was a *disaster*.

He wanted to raise Bennett Schuyler from the dead so he could wring his fool neck.

"You can't actually make me do what you want

just because you want it," Annika was informing him. "I don't work for you. This thundery, growly, alpha male thing probably works really well for you in your capacity as CEO of all the things. But you're not the CEO of *me*."

Ranieri had the bizarre urge to put his hands—

But no. He rejected that urge with every part of him. There would be no hands. And if, later, he found himself questioning the fact that he had imagined sinking his own deep into the bedraggled mess of her silky brown hair... Well.

That was a horror he did not intend to delve into too deeply now. Or ever. Not all questions required answers.

"It is interesting you would mention my position as CEO," he said, a bit forbiddingly. Maybe a little ruthlessly. He reminded himself that he did not have to play these games. That he was choosing to engage with Bennett Schuyler's unfathomable directions, to serve his own ends. His own appalling sentimentality, perhaps. "If I were you, Annika, I would bear in mind the difference that exists between us. As far as I'm aware, that museum of yours is the only thing that you could possibly do with yourself. Having made yourself essentially unhirable in any other capacity."

She looked unmoved by any ruthlessness or forbidding tones on his part. "That's quite a leap. I

haven't actually attempted to get myself hired anywhere else. But if I did, I'm sure that I would be an
excellent candidate. For any number of reasons."

"You would not be," he said shortly. "On the
other hand, while I would like to keep my position
at Schuyler Corporation, it is not essential. At the
end of the day, Annika, I am me."

She blinked at that. And then, with no apparent
understanding of the danger she was in, she rolled
her eyes.

Those impossibly green eyes. Directly at him.

Ranieri ground his teeth together, but pushed on.
"I can go anywhere. Most corporations would sing
hosannas at my approach. I can see that you want to
argue this." And it pleased him, perhaps more than
it should, when her green eyes blazed but her mouth
snapped shut. "But once again, that is the function
of arrogance. Yours, not mine. This is reality. You
want to be very, very careful here, I think."

He had the impression that she wanted to rage
at him, and found himself intrigued by the notion.
What would rage look like on her? She was already
flushed. It made her cheeks brighter, and he found
himself wondering if that flush extended all over.

Clearly, he needed a woman. Badly. It was obviously an emergency if he was lowering himself
to imagining *flushes* on Annika Schuyler's body.

And maybe it was even more lowering than that,

because when she pulled in a breath, he found himself tensing. Everywhere.

As if he wanted her to shift all of this into a different place. A place of anger. *Passion,* something in him whispered. *Isn't that what you wanted?*

But instead, she let that breath out again. And though he didn't see her move, he had the impression that she lengthened, somehow. Ranieri had never thought her the least bit elegant or graceful in any way, and yet she had the look of it, then. As if there was something innately graceful about her when she chose to show it. As if, when she pleased, she could posture up like any other debutante worth her salt.

He would not forget that.

"I'll need you to be very clear here," she said quietly. "I want to make sure I'm understanding you completely."

"I think you understand me just fine," he replied carelessly. Mostly to see if the tone he used brought out the red in her cheeks, and it did. "But for the sake of argument, Annika, why don't we say simply that as far as you and I are concerned, I am your CEO."

And surely he was much less of a man than he should have been, because when she sputtered at that, he enjoyed it.

Not because he'd clearly won another negotiation, so of course he liked it. He always liked winning, or he wouldn't make sure to do it so often.

But this victory felt personal.

Ranieri decided he would hold that against her, too.

CHAPTER THREE

ANNIKA DIDN'T RECALL agreeing to anything.

She knew full well she hadn't.

But her actual, verbal agreement was unnecessary, apparently. Because Ranieri took control. He looked as if he meant to laugh at her, there in that conference room where she'd so foolishly believed for a giddy moment that she might have the upper hand.

When, as far she knew when it involved this man, no one ever had the upper hand. There was a reason he was feared and loathed and revered and admired wherever he went.

"You might consider putting your shoes back on," he told her in that icy way of his, perfectly calibrated to make her feel as ashamed of herself as she had when she was a teenage girl besieged by her own hormones. What an unpleasant reminder of those dark years. "Unless, of course, it is your goal to impress upon the entirety of this law firm that you are, at heart, distressingly bohemian unto your embarrassing soul."

His expression suggested that if she took that route, she might find herself in even less of a good position concerning her father's final wishes.

She could have argued about that. But it felt like she was aiming for nothing but a Pyrrhic victory and she wasn't in the mood for self-immolation on such a tough day. Annika bit her tongue and kept her protestations to herself. She slid her feet back into her shoes, tried to pretend they weren't the torture devices she knew they were, and then limped out after Ranieri. He merely stalked to the conference room door in his obviously handcrafted Italian shoes—likely made for him personally, with love, by teams of rapturous artisans—flung it open, and somehow summoned the entire team of lawyers to his side. Simply by appearing, she had to think. Because she would have heard him if he'd yelled, snapped his fingers, or did whatever it was he did to make them all dance to his tune.

He exists, a voice in her said glumly. *That's the beginning and the end of everything, including you.*

Annika was not a glum person, generally speaking. That was why she was good at what she did, getting people to donate money to keep the museum running smoothly with an eye toward a Schuyler-less future one day, keeping the staff happy, and making sure it remained a desirable destination in a city with museums for every mood.

Yet her father's will and his demands had her feeling pretty distinctly glum, all the same.

Ranieri barked out commands, the lawyers scuttled about taking notes and aggressively agreeing to everything he said—big surprise—and the next thing she knew, Annika was seated in the back of a gleaming limo, gliding through Manhattan traffic as if even the usual Midtown snarls did not dare keep this man waiting.

Annika didn't ask where they were going. Because she had the distinct impression that he wanted her to ask. Likely so he could have the pleasure of telling her, which would make it even more clear that he was in control of what was happening here.

She refused to play along. And she decided there and then that she did not have it in her to cater to this man's pleasures.

And then had to sit there, contemplating his pleasures, such as they were, as she thought about what that might mean for a man like him. A man who looked so *physical* in clothes that made a great many other men look like they were playing dress-up or trying to do a James Bond impression.

Ranieri looked as if he was the man all James Bonds had tried, and failed, to emulate.

More she had to wonder what *his pleasures* might mean for her, the woman who hadn't actually agreed to marry him…but was marrying him anyway.

Surely he was only talking about sex and passion in general terms, because he planned to put on this act of his. Surely he had no intention of…experimenting with such things. With Annika.

She fought, hard, to keep her expression as impassive as humanly possible. Even while her entire body seemed to burn, like she'd immolated herself after all.

Still, it was impossible not to show some hint of surprise when he stopped…at a bank.

How prosaic.

"Are you planning to fling money at the people who dare to question this unholy alliance?" she asked. "That will really get you in all the papers."

Entertaining that image in her head was a lot more amusing than the other one. The one involving pleasure and sex and *passion*.

Ranieri only slanted a dark gaze her way. Just a glance, and yet it fairly seethed with reproof. "Wait here."

His driver opened his door and he exited the back of the car without any heaving around or fighting for purchase on the back of the seat in front of him. Not Ranieri. He merely rose from within, as if he was inevitable. As if he had more power and flexibility in one toe than most mortals held in the whole of their bodies.

And there she was again, thinking about bodies.

His body, to be precise.

Alone in the back seat, she allowed herself a little breather. A little chance to check in with herself. Nothing this morning had gone as she had intended it to go. So now, by herself, she could finally accept that really, she was just a mess of too many feelings.

The very thing her father had always despaired of most in her.

Emotion is a trap, my girl, Bennett had liked to rumble at her. *Be better than that, and if you can't, do please refrain from chewing your legs off in public.*

She found herself smiling at that, even now. Even here. Because that had been her dad to a T. Gruff. Blunt. Funny.

Annika missed him dreadfully. At least while he'd been in his coma, she'd still been able to see him. To sit by his bed and tell him about her life. To hold his hand and love him.

Maybe the real truth was that despite everything she'd been told by every single doctor who had spoken to her at length about her father's condition, she had still believed that somehow, he would beat this. That despite everything, he would rise up again, take his rightful place, and these past five years would be washed away as if they'd never been.

Maybe she still hadn't quite accepted that he was really, truly dead.

The funeral hadn't helped. It had been packed full of all the sorts of people her father had enjoyed but who she always found so overwhelming. Mostly because they spent all their time speaking out of both sides of their faces at once. One side to express their condolences, and the other to sneer down their noses at her. Even in her grief, she had been keenly aware that she did not live up to expectations.

That poor, sad creature, she'd heard one of her father's friends murmur. *It's hard to imagine a less likely heir to Bennett.*

Maybe he died to escape the shame, the friend's snide female companion had tittered.

Though Annika almost laughed, sitting there in the back seat of a limousine waiting for Ranieri to return, as she imagined all the snooty people she knew and the reactions they were going to have when this got out. When Ranieri told the world he was actually marrying the hopeless, sad, *shameful* Annika Schuyler.

For *sex*, no less.

That really did make her laugh, no matter how she tried to put her hands over her mouth and muffle the sound. And the more she tried to muffle herself, because even she knew it wasn't good manners to snort with laughter when the driver could hear her, the louder she got. The more hysterical.

Then, after she'd laughed a bit, it turned into something a little closer to sobbing, and she understood that. She understood that grief was physical in a thousand ways and much like the flu, it would come as it chose. Stay as long as it liked. And leave when it was ready, not a moment before.

Yet when Ranieri swung back into the car, she spent a few moments congratulating herself on having stopped the sobbing before his return. Then questioned herself. Why hadn't she run off? It was the principle of the thing. It wasn't as if she could run away from what was happening. She knew that. But it would have been nice to not simply…surrender to this man. And so easily.

Annika was certain that was what everyone did. She was certain he expected no less, in fact. He was the sort of man who expected that everywhere he went, mass genuflections should follow. Really, she should have walked off for the sheer joy of interrupting his arrogance for a few moments.

The way he'd reappeared had been a shock. Or maybe that was simply him. The door had opened and there was the usual assault of a New York City street. The noise, the smells, the rush of people.

But then Ranieri was in the middle of all that,

somehow rougher and rawer than anything around him. Somehow more intense than the rush and whirl of Manhattan itself.

"Did they not give you your bags of money?" she asked him, because he certainly wasn't carrying any. She blew out a dramatic sort of breath. "Don't they know who you are?"

He ignored that. He thumped his hand on the roof of the car, clearly an order to his driver because sure enough, the car pulled out into traffic again.

"I'm having my people prepare the appropriate statement," he told her coolly. Maybe she ought to have been grateful that he seemed to be so focused on keeping this businesslike. Then again, that was just his personality, as long as she'd known him. All business. All power games. That was the Ranieri Furlan promise. "It will be delivered to media outlets within the hour."

"Dare I ask which statement that is?" Annika felt that uncontrollable laughter well up inside her again and did her best to stuff it back down, because she doubted he would react well to it. "Is it the one where you're the boss of me?"

He turned then, shifting his body so that he could face her across the back seat. His golden gaze slammed into her, so hard that if she hadn't been looking at him, and perfectly aware where his hands were, she might have thought that he'd pushed her back against the seat with one of them. That was how it felt.

"I hope you're enjoying these witticisms of yours," he said in that soft way of his that really wasn't soft at all. "Someone should. I will suggest to you that it would be better if you got them out of your system here in private. I doubt they will play as well on the national stage."

"Goodness," she said weakly. "Will there be a *stage*?"

"Our engagement will be news, Annika. I am news. And so, I suppose, are you. In your way."

"That almost feels like it was supposed to be a compliment." She shook her head at him. "And yet you couldn't quite commit to it, could you?"

He looked at her in that manner of his that she'd experienced entirely too many times over the past five years when he'd been the guardian she neither wanted nor needed. As if he found being in her presence required so much patience, *so much*, that it nearly wrecked him as he struggled to provide it. As if even gazing at her required a level of forbearance most men could not possibly achieve.

There were times she found it amusing. Today was not one of those times.

"My grandmother, like most of the women in my family, had an innate elegance and exquisite style." He bit off those words as if they were bullets, but not necessarily aimed at her. "She consulted the finest jewelers in Paris for this ring, which I bestow upon you in the hope that you will rise to meet it, and it is not so much…"

Something in her curled around and around, a little too much like the sort of shame ruthlessly curated women at funerals thought she ought to feel. The kind of shame that made her angry, because it wasn't hers. *She* liked herself. Annika clung to that anger, that red-hot burst of something like defiance, because it was better than the alternative.

"Pearls before swine?" she threw at him. "Is that what you meant to say?"

Ranieri's mouth went grim. He reached into his pocket and pulled out a small velvet box, then flipped it open.

And Annika was no stranger to beautiful jewelry. The museum was full of it. Her sweet mother had left Annika all of hers, and she treasured every piece. She told herself stories about the various jewels, and had, when she was younger, excavated every known photograph of her mother so she could wear her jewelry in the same manner. But it wasn't only her mother's jewelry. As the last in her family, she had been handed down beautiful heirlooms from every side. Wearing them, or even gazing at them, made her feel closer to all the women who had gone before her.

But the ring in that small box Ranieri held was in another category altogether.

For one thing, it was mammoth.

"Is that a ring or a life preserver?" she breathed.

"It is a one of a kind, sixteen-carat Asscher-cut diamond without peer," he growled at her.

Annika had the strangest notion that she'd offended him, and then he was reaching over and taking her hand, notably without his usual patience, tried however sorely. And she knew what he was doing. There was only one thing he could be doing. Still, something inside her shivered with a certain wild anticipation that suggested she actually thought—

But of course she didn't. *Of course* she didn't think anything of the kind. She knew he wasn't *holding her hand*, just as she knew this wasn't real. He wasn't *actually* proposing to her.

Most importantly, she didn't *want* him to touch her. She'd never wanted that.

Annika felt the cool touch of the platinum band as he slid it over her knuckle, then into place. As *into place* as anything could be when the stone attached to the band was the size of a golf ball. It was obscene. It was outrageous.

It was really very beautiful, she thought in the next moment, almost against her will. It seemed to float over her hand, catching all the September

light and making flares out of it. The diamond itself was cut to look like a hall of mirrors. As if she
could simply sink into it and disappear forever...

And then both she and Ranieri seemed to notice,
in the same moment, that the ring fit her perfectly.
Almost as if it had been made for her.

Annika's gaze flew to his, and just like that, it
was as if they were somewhere else. No longer in
this car, careening through the New York streets.
They were somewhere else, a place where there was
only her hand in his, that ring on her finger huge
enough to take out an eye, and yet all she could concentrate on was the gold looking back at her. The
gold that seemed to spear straight through her, fill-
ing her up, *changing* her—

"Congratulations," Ranieri bit out, breaking the
spell. His voice dark. Grim, even. A sensation that
matched moved through her, a deep shudder. A dark
knowing. A foreboding, she was sure. "We are now
engaged."

As if he was handing down a prison sentence.

Ten momentous days later, Annika made her way
through yet another depressingly well-heeled crowd,
all too aware that she had been to more parties in
the past week and a half than in the entire previous five years.

She had discovered many things. That she did

not, in fact, enjoy New York society parties, for example. This one had taken over the whole of an industrial loft that, as far she could tell, existed entirely for its floor-to-ceiling windows with lazy views all around. Sometimes, she was given to understand, there were art shows here. But tonight it was all the same sort of people doing the same sort of thing.

New York's finest and brightest and snobbiest, too, raising money for some or other cause célèbre.

Annika had gotten her fill of them quickly. By the time Ranieri had dropped her home the afternoon of their engagement, such as it was, it seemed that all of New York had heard the news. Her phone had been ringing off the hook, and her phone never rang off the hook. It barely rang at all. Mostly because her friends knew that she preferred a text. Still, she'd locked herself away in the sprawling family apartment on Fifth Avenue that rambled over three floors, felt like a house, and was an excellent place to take refuge from the world.

She'd left her phone on the hall table so it couldn't bug her and if it weren't for the incredible piece of hardware on her hand, she might have been able to convince herself that nothing had happened.

Except the next day, far too early, there had been an impatient hammering on her door. Not the door to the apartment, the door to her bedroom.

When she'd opened it, expecting one of her father's staff members to inform her that the ceiling had caved in or some such emergency, it was instead Ranieri.

What are you...? she'd started to ask him, bewildered and so beside herself that she'd barely even noticed that while *he* was completely dressed in another one of those suits of his that really should have been against the law, *she* was not dressed at all. She wore a giant, shapeless T-shirt that came down almost to her knees.

Our first event as an engaged couple is tonight, he had informed her, his golden eyes glittering. *You'll understand that I must insist steps are taken to make you presentable.*

Annika liked to look back on that moment and tell herself it was because she was still half-asleep—and not entirely understanding why he was in her apartment in the first place—that she'd simply taken that at face value.

Because what had followed was one humiliation after another. It made the sight she must have presented to him—hair doing God only knew what and that sad tent of a T-shirt—fade into insignificance. What she would give now to fume about the fact the doorman should never have let him in. Even though she knew that wasn't entirely fair. Throughout her father's long convalescence, Ranieri had been a near-daily visitor. Of course they had let him in.

Her phone had been ringing when she'd come home, but she'd ignored it. So it hadn't been until she'd walked out of the apartment building on Fifth Avenue the following morning, in Ranieri's company, that she got a taste of how everything had changed.

It was awful.

Annika was now engaged to the most eligible man in…maybe anywhere. And she hated it. There were cameras everywhere. Flashbulbs and unpleasant men shouting her name. The ring itself caused a commotion. Almost as much of a commotion as Ranieri had caused inside when he'd discovered that she had not slept with it on.

I never sleep in my jewelry, she'd told him, scowling at him when she'd finally had enough coffee—and had found enough actual clothes—to deal with him.

I suggest you learn, he had retorted. *Quickly.*

In that way he had that wasn't a suggestion at all.

He had dragged her off and delivered her to what appeared to be a pleasant brownstone not far from the neighborhood where she'd grown up. Except it turned out it was far more pernicious than that. It was no family home, it was the modern New York version of the modiste. Ranieri steered her to one of the house's salons, and then—after conferring for some time—left her to the tender mercies of the women who worked there, all of them dressed in black and possessed of the kind of sharp gazes that suggested they existed entirely on cigarettes and spite.

What they did was provide her with an appropriate wardrobe. That was the word they had kept using. *Appropriate*.

I already have clothes, she had complained before he'd left. *Lots of clothes, actually.*

Ranieri had not rolled his eyes, though he had done something that she could only describe as the Italian version of *almost* rolling his eyes, but not quite. *My woman will be held to a different standard, obviously. It is the* kind *of clothes. Not just anything will do. And if we're lucky, the clothes themselves will lend you an air of elegance.*

It had taken her a while to work out that when he said that, he meant the sort of elegance she did not possess already. And she wanted to be angry about that. She did.

But after ten days with the paparazzi in her face, she was forced to contend with the realities of her life. Like the fact she was so klutzy. Clumsy, even. Then there were all the ways she was incapable of doing her hair in the way people who contended with the paparazzi needed to. She kept falling over her own two feet, her hair a mess, the way she always did. And it was disconcerting to suddenly have an audience.

An audience that liked to take pictures of her looking foolish, not that it was hard.

Meanwhile, Ranieri kept dragging her to events. And it had been one thing when she was her father's hostess or date. People had been a little more indulgent, not that she had entirely recognized that indulgence at the time. Back then, she would make idle conversation with her father's acquaintances, but when he decided to start talking business, she would excuse herself.

And not so she could mingle with the sorts of people who attended these parties. Perish the thought. Her actual friends did not attend New York City social events. If they did, they wouldn't be her friends. At such events Annika preferred to wander off on her own. She had befriended a great many caterers and actors that way, which meant, over time, she got into the best restaurants and went backstage at the best shows. She'd also seen a number of unexpected views, from unique angles. She'd also seen a lot of people doing things they probably shouldn't have been doing, but anyway, none of that mattered now, because being with Ranieri was like being in the spotlight.

A glaring, endless spotlight that was as blinding as it was hot.

It was bad enough that she could never pull off looking sophisticated, while he oozed it with his usual edgy effortlessness. There were other hazards. Most of them of the feminine variety.

There were entirely too many sophisticated, not-a-hair-out-of-place type women who circled her like sharks at these things. All of them seemed to take her engagement to Ranieri personally. Especially because he'd made no secret of the fact that they intended to wed at the end of the month. Within two weeks, now. She assumed that was why all of them tried, in various ways, to mean girl her whenever they saw her.

No one, in or out of a tabloid, could believe that Ranieri Furlan was marrying *her*.

Most people suspected she was pregnant.

But being assumed pregnant usually meant that people had accepted the notion that she and Ranieri had something between them. That they'd actually had sex. There were a lot of others who couldn't quite get there.

Tonight, for example, Annika had been caught against her will in a tedious conversation with three debutantes she wished she could pretend she didn't know. But she did. They'd all gone to private school together. One was on her fifth engagement. Another was on her second husband, having rid herself of the first when he was stripped of his royal title— though she let it be known that she was already in the market for her third. The other debutante—really more of a socialite, since they weren't eighteen any longer—spent more time in the tabloids than some actual Hollywood celebrities. And what they'd wanted to talk about was how much they'd desperately wanted to be her friend all these years.

Lies, of course. Which she'd known even before the much-engaged one felt the need to make a few pointed comments about the rock on Annika's hand.

I've always preferred a classic style myself, she'd said, though the look in her face was one of pure envy. *But I suppose that if I'd managed to land Ranieri Furlan, I'd also want evidence of my triumph to beam out into outer space.*

What Annika wished she could have said was that she didn't particularly *want* to be engaged to Ranieri in the first place, and certainly didn't view it as a triumph. What she'd done was hold out her left hand and gaze down at the enormous stone as if she'd never seen it before, then had glanced at the "classic" stone on the other woman's hand.

Which, she realized only after she'd done it, might possibly have been seen as some kind of… flex.

The reality was that Annika was no good at these

games. She didn't like playing them. Especially because Ranieri had gone and told anyone who would listen that their engagement so soon after her father's death was all about passion.

He actually kept saying that, repeatedly. *Passion.*

She'd heard him talking about it some more tonight, though she had attempted to give him a wide berth as she'd headed out of the main loft space. *At a certain point, passion can no longer be denied,* she'd heard him say. *Mea culpa.*

The man was terrifyingly focused. It wasn't enough that he'd taken it upon himself to *My Fair Lady* her. It wasn't enough that he'd followed that up by hiring her a personal stylist that she didn't want, so that now she had to contend with being followed around by the steel-eyed Marissa, who was always trying to *do things* with eye pencils and *foundation,* whatever that was.

I will have your things moved into my loft in Tribeca, he had told her that first day, after she'd spent entirely too long being measured and then forced to try on clothes and prance about in them. At least she hadn't had to do it in front of him, and then he hadn't even looked up from whatever it was he was doing on his laptop when he'd collected her. She shouldn't have cared. *Tomorrow, I think.*

I have a much better idea, she had retorted, feeling stung. And maybe something like overwhelmed, though she had chosen not to ask herself why, exactly, that was. *Why don't you move into my apartment, which has the added benefit of numerous floors we can put between us?*

His golden gaze had swept over her and left her feeling… Not shaken, not really. It was more a quivering, deep inside. *I think not. That would not give off the right impression at all. You will move in with me.*

She had, because she knew as well as he did that any refusal to cooperate with him could be leveraged against her. And with everything around her changing so rapidly, and so against her will, she couldn't lose Schuyler House.

It was the only thing she had left.

Which was why she'd reacted the way she did to Ranieri's nightly round of ultimatums tonight.

The wedding will take place a week from Sunday, he had informed her on the way to tonight's fundraiser. Looking as bored as ever. *I have already had your dress made.*

Of course you have. She had stared out the window, toying with the ring on her hand and making it flash against passing cabs like a beacon. Possibly a cry for help. *No need to consult me. I'm only the bride.*

He had ignored that the way he ignored most of the things she said. Sometimes she thought that if he had his way, she would stay tucked away in the guest room in his loft where he'd installed her. It had exposed brick and a sumptuous bathtub, a killer view, and every night she went to sleep and dreamed of him.

It was not ideal.

But then, none of this was.

I'm thinking we should just run down to City Hall and be done with it, she'd told him earlier. *No muss, no fuss.*

And, bonus, it wouldn't feel like a real wedding.

Absolutely not, he had replied. He'd looked up then, that gaze of his far too steady. *We will get married here in New York City. Where both of us are known so well. We will not get married at City Hall. I'm thinking your beloved Schuyler House will do.*

She'd sat bolt upright. *No. That's out of the question.*

It is not a request, Annika, he had replied in that dark, stirring way of his. *For one thing, there are very few appropriate venues on such short notice. For another, it is no secret that it is a place you love. What else could possibly lend this enterprise the patina of truth?*

Truth does not have a patina, she had tossed back at him, surprised at the rush of red-hot temper inside her. Surprised, but not enough to tamp it down or hide it. *Truth is truth, no patina required. Why am I unsurprised that you don't know that?*

That's very earnest, I am sure. And very naive. He'd shaken his head. *There are lingering whispers about us, as I'm sure you know. Getting married in a place that has such resonance can only put those to rest. That and a honeymoon.*

We're not having a honeymoon, *Ranieri,* she had yelped. She had actually *yelped* at him. *Honeymoons are for people who need to loll about on beaches and have marital relations. That is not us.*

She'd regretted that, instantly. It was bad enough when he traipsed around Manhattan, speaking endlessly about *passion* to all and sundry. They did not speak of it themselves. That seemed… like adding fuel to the fire, at the very least. Foolish, in other words.

And then, in the back seat of a limousine, it seemed something far worse, far more dangerous, than simply foolish.

It almost seemed like a dare. Or like arson. Annika couldn't breathe.

She'd never in her life been so happy to arrive at a party she already knew she would dislike. And now, having managed to slip away from the main room of the party, she made her way out to one of the balconies. This one looked north, and she took a moment to sigh a bit and look at this marvelous, magical city she'd called home her whole life. New York was unknowable and familiar at the same time. New York always rose, no matter how it fell.

Staring out at the city, she felt something stir inside her.

She'd been going about this all wrong. She'd been so surprised by Ranieri's ferocity and command since the reading of the will, especially after the milder guardianship years, and he was pressing his advantage, wasn't he?

But then, she should have expected he would. That was who he was.

The stark reality was that she had only a little bit of time left to get him to break this engagement. If he was the one to break it off, he would lose the company and she would lose nothing. More importantly, she would be free.

She'd been so busy letting him trot her about from stylist to fashion house to party, each stop more soul killing than the last. And she'd gone along with it, because implicit in every ultimatum he handed her was the fact that if she refused, he could report that she wasn't playing along. He could make the case that she was not abiding by the rules her own father had set out.

But there were levels of compliance.

And two could play this game.

She stood there, looking out at the gleaming, glittering city. Always so many bright lights, from red brake lights on the streets below to all the thousands of lit-up windows, so many people and so many lives piled on top and around each other.

Surely there was no passion greater than this.

But that word echoed around inside her differently now. Maybe because she'd heard Ranieri use it so many times. Maybe because she finally felt as if her head was a little bit more clear, at last. Out here in the cool air of a late September night.

Because he wanted to get married at Schuyler House and she wanted to keep Schuyler House as it had always been. Hers, alone. Not marked by him the way everything else in her life was. And yes, maybe she'd thought that it might be nice to get married there someday, but not to him.

Never to *him*.

But if she didn't want this to happen, she had only one path forward.

Passion, she thought to herself.

Maybe it was time that she gave Ranieri some of that passion he kept going on about. A lot of passion. More passion than he could handle—and none of it violating the terms of her father's will. Or involving sex, no matter what she dreamed about, curled up in his guest room in Tribeca.

All these people in his glittering, shallow world already treated her like she was some kind of loon.

Annika smiled at her beloved city. Why not act the part?

She couldn't think of a better way to get him to end their engagement, so she could keep Schuyler House to herself.

And free her from him, once and for all.

CHAPTER FOUR

RANIERI WAS AN hour into an important, if some-
what tedious, meeting when the conference room
door burst open. His immediate assumption was
that the building was on fire, for there could be no
other reason his people would disturb him. They
knew better.

It took him long moments of staring down the
length of the conference table, over the laptops and
stacks of documents everywhere, to make sense
of the fact that the person who stood there in the
open door was not his long-suffering personal assistant, the competent Gregory, though he could see
Gregory himself out in the hall, looking horrified.

The person who had tossed the door open was,
improbably, Annika.

"I don't want to interrupt," she trilled, while
doing exactly that.

And Ranieri was not one to countenance acts

of defiance. He insisted on respect and reasonable obedience in all things and, when he received both, he was perhaps a demanding boss, but fair. Always fair.

But what was *fair* when it came to this woman who had been foisted upon him? The truth was, he had no earthly idea what to do with Annika.

He had spent a significant amount of money outfitting her appropriately. He'd had a number of stylists convene upon her, taking the raw materials she presented and working their magic. And he had to admit it had been worth it. Gone was her typical bedraggled look. Ranieri had been quietly pleased to find that while she would never be knocking anyone off the cover of *Vogue*, Bennett Schuyler's daughter was, in fact, capable of looking reasonably put together. And that was a relief. It made it slightly less inconceivable that she had somehow captured his interest.

Yet she was still Annika.

Today she wore a dress in a shade of teal he would normally have considered loud, but it flattered her. It flattered her too much, perhaps. He hadn't expected that. The first night he'd picked her up after the stylists had taken their liberties with her, he'd been…surprised. That was the word, surely. He'd been *surprised* to discover that beneath the careless hair, the wrinkled linens, and the voluminous cardigans she liked to drape all over herself in the colder months, Annika actually possessed a figure.

He told himself he was noticing such things for strategic purposes, nothing more.

Today, for example, he was merely noticing that the teal dress was expertly tailored to flatter her surprisingly generous breasts as well as the tiny waist he hadn't realized she possessed. The flare of her hips below was another surprise, and one he had revisited—privately—a few too many times since she'd moved into his loft.

In his head, that was.

Her hair was twisted back this morning, not falling down this way and that. She still wore what he supposed was a version of one of her ratty cardigans, but at least this version whispered of quiet sophistication as it draped behind her like a cape.

And yet he realized that all the usual disheveled energy came directly from her. Even when, objectively speaking, he could find no specific fault with her appearance, she gave off the distinct impression that there was at least one.

Then again, perhaps the problem was that she was bearing before her a potted plant with raucously pink flowers.

Ranieri blinked, certain he was imagining that—but no.

His newly minted fiancée was indeed charging into his conference room, holding before her a large, potted plant. The pot itself appeared to be wrapped in something, a kind of foil perhaps, but it was magenta. Which matched the oversize bow wrapped around it. And yet those pinks were a different pink from that of the exuberant, round flowers.

Ranieri had never been in an actual fistfight, despite the many years he'd spent training in martial arts like Brazilian jujitsu. He had never *actually* been attacked. And yet this moment felt the closest he'd ever been to an all-out assault.

He did not dare look around the table at his colleagues and business associates. The strained silence in the room told him all he needed to know about their reactions. It was obvious they matched his own.

"I just wanted to take this opportunity to bring you this plant," Annika was saying brightly. She swept to the head of the table and stopped before him, then smiled.

Fatuously, to his mind.

"Our passion cannot be contained," she said, that smile widening, her voice almost certainly loud enough to carry down the length of the hall outside. "How I've longed these last years to tell the whole world what we mean to each other!"

"I am delighted," Ranieri managed to say, without sounding *entirely* as if he had glass in his mouth. "But as you can see, I'm also rather busy."

Annika responded by thunking down the pot before him, a little too close to his laptop for his liking.

"I saw it and I knew you had to have it," she told him, an intensity in her voice that he had never heard before. Probably because she was putting it on. This close, he could see the cool amusement in her green gaze. Then she frowned slightly as she looked around the table. "Pink flowers symbolize love, of course."

It was a table filled with titans of industry and the sharpest business minds around, yet they all nodded as if they had come here today to immerse themselves in bloody floriography. Ranieri might have laughed, it was so absurd, except Annika swung her gaze back to him.

"I know how important your job is to you," she said. Intensely. "And as the woman who loves you best and most, I want to support you while you toil away, making money and then making more money, ha-ha-ha."

He stared at her in stark astonishment as she really dug into that fake laugh.

That had to be the end of it—but no. She wasn't done.

"But of course, my sweet Ranieri Berry," she

said, and he was certain he was dreaming then.
Because there was no possibility that this woman
had just lapsed into baby talk in the middle of the
delicate negotiation. There was no possibility that
she had just called him by a pet name so saccharine
and nauseating that he was not entirely certain how
it was the entire conference table hadn't lapsed into
a sugar coma. He wished he had. "*Of course* I miss
you so much while you're here. So I found you this
wonderful dahlia that will bloom, pink and bright,
like our love."

Because, yes, there was a darker place. A lower
level of horror.

"It will bloom here at the office and you'll think
of our love. You will care for it and tend to it while
we are parted." Then the ghastly woman had the
gall to beam at him. "Won't you?"

Ranieri stared at the explosion of pink before
him. Then he lifted his gaze and glared around the
table, daring anyone seated at it to so much as smirk
in his direction.

As one, every person there dropped their gaze.

"You don't like it," Annika breathed, as if she
had, just that very moment, watched him kick a
puppy. Her puppy, when he knew full well she did
not have one. Then as he gazed at her in his continued appalled astonishment, she stuck out her lower
lip like a child. And if he wasn't mistaken, set it to

trembling. "You hate it, and that must mean you hate me. And what does that say about our love, Ranieri?"

Her voice grew shriller with every word. And Ranieri could see her intentions all over her face. The quivering lip. That look in her eyes, like she was fully prepared to go for broke.

He honestly had no idea what he would do if she broke down and sobbed.

Which he could tell she had every intention of doing.

Ranieri stood then, briskly enough that it made his oh-so-charming fiancée blink and take a step back, which was the first reasonable thing she'd done since arriving here today.

"*Amore*, you are overset," he murmured in a low voice, and then, moving quickly, he scooped up the ridiculous pink plant in one arm while adroitly maneuvering his other arm around Annika's shoulders.

Then he made what he hoped was a soothing sort of noise as he walked her—marched her—out of the conference room.

And this was not the time to notice what it felt like to have her that close to him. He didn't touch her, as a rule. Especially not since he'd been bludgeoned by the hourglass figure she'd apparently been hiding all this time behind shapeless clothing. But it was impossible not to notice a few too many things about her as he swiftly escorted her from the room. That delicate scent that he tried to tell himself was hair product of some kind, but he knew better. It was a lotion she put on her skin when she was alone, perhaps, or maybe it was just her—a faint hint of something sweeter and better than the finest vanilla.

Out in the hall, Ranieri kept moving, striding with her toward his office, where he could deal with her without so many eyes on them. He kept his arm clamped around her shoulders, because he was passing too many curious underlings—all of whom pretended not to be studying them with avid interest.

He caught a glimpse of the spectacle they made as he marched them past one of the glossy interior walls, and gritted his teeth at the absurdity of it all. He felt like a dancing bear at the circus, which he assumed was her intent. But he was fairly certain she caught that same glimpse of their ungainly procession, because her delicate shoulders began to shake.

And when he ushered her into his office and then released her, he could see that she was laughing after all. Ranieri told himself that was marginally better than if she was crying.

This time, he wasn't surprised when his temper swept through him, but he still had no intention of giving in to it. He left her by the door, because he needed to stop touching her, and stalked across the long, stark room that was built to be a clean, cool antidote to the busy city outside his windows. Then he set the infernal plant down on his desk with a thud.

And he took his time turning back to face her, because he could hear the little noises she was making, as if trying to stifle her laughter with her hands.

When he finally turned, that was exactly what she was doing. And for moment, he stopped and stared. Because she was so outrageous, he told himself.

But he knew it was something else. The teal dress and her hair swept back, though a dark tendril had worked its way free. In contrast to her usual messy-hair moments, this actually looked…inviting. Or maybe it was the fact that she was laughing, that she had bent over a little with one arm wrapped around her waist, which only seemed to call more attention to that astonishing figure of hers.

He really needed to get a hold of himself. It was not part of his plan to be attracted to Annika. He intended to marry her, not pant about after her.

The thought of panting after anyone was egregious enough that it sobered him. Quickly. He was Ranieri Furlan. He did not *pant*.

"Do you have any idea what that display will

likely cost me?" he asked her, his voice wintry enough that she ought to have checked for snow.

She straightened, still laughing, and did not appear overly moved by his question. Or concerned about a sudden interior snowfall. Instead, she wiped at her eyes, still laughing softly. "Good thing, then, that you have more money than God."

"I cannot imagine what could possibly have possessed you," he began again, even more furious.

This time, when her green eyes met his from across the length of his office, they were shrewd. "Are you embarrassed? Angry, outraged, any or all of the above? Whatever will you do, Ranieri?" Her lips curved. "Or should I call you, Ranieri Berry?"

"If I ever hear that sickening phrase uttered aloud again, I will not be responsible for my actions, Annika. I hope you are hearing me."

"I'll be certain to say it in front of the paparazzi, then." And she only smiled deeper when he tensed. "Is it too much for you yet? Are you ready to say uncle?"

Ranieri was familiar with that odd North American saying, though he would never have used it himself. Particularly not when his own uncles had embodied the very worst of the Furlan pride and all that entailed. It had gotten one of them killed. The other was currently a shell of a man, shuffling about in the tatters of his former glory somewhere outside Firenze.

But the meaning wasn't lost on him.

"Do you think embarrassing yourself in my office will lead me to surrender?" He didn't quite laugh. Not quite. "Oh, Annika. You don't know me very well, do you?"

Her green eyes gleamed. But all she did was nod toward the pink monstrosity now cluttering up his glass desk.

"Enjoy the embodiment of our love," she said softly. "And don't let me keep you from the rest of your very important meeting. *Amore*."

And he had no choice but to stay where he was as she turned around and sauntered out of his office. Actually *sauntered*, with entirely too much confidence for a woman who had once limped into the reading of her father's will.

He had no choice because he knew that if he went after her he would put his hands on her. And once that happened, he was not certain what would come next. And this was his place of business. It was as close to a cathedral as he got.

Because he could tell himself that what was storming around inside him was temper. Sheer outrage. That he was tensed up and ready to fight, that was all. But in all his years of martial arts training to prepare for such moments, one part of him had never been tense. And yet somehow, it was his sex that felt the neediest in the wake of Annika's performance.

All of that required him to stay where he was, seething and furious, until he got a hold of himself.

Only then could he go back into the conference room and attempt to salvage his meeting from her pink-planted wreckage.

When he got back to Tribeca that evening, Ranieri's mood was precarious. He'd managed to negotiate the deal he wanted, but with a bit more in the way of concessions than he normally allowed.

It was entirely Annika's fault.

He nodded at the doorman, then strode to his private elevator and tried to prepare himself for the woman who had not simply disrupted his morning meeting—in an epic fashion—but had haunted him the rest of the day. He'd kept thinking he could smell that faint scent, all hers. He'd kept remembering the feel of her body so close to his when he'd had that arm wrapped around her.

Ranieri had been distracted. He was never distracted.

At least he could take some solace in the fact that she was in no way comfortable in his home. Or so he assumed from the stiff way she moved around in it, always acting as if it was a great sacrifice on her part to live in one of the most sought-after addresses in the city.

She'd lived here a week exactly now, he thought as the elevator rose at its sedate pace, when he had never intended to cohabitate with anyone. In the past it had always been clear to him that was necessary to cut ties with his various mistresses when they'd made too many noises about wanting to move in, stay over, clear a little space for their things, and other such slippery slopes that led straight to all the places he did not wish to go.

But Bennett Schuyler had wanted them living together within a week, so here they were.

He could admit, when he got past the enduring fury of the plant incident earlier, that Annika had thus far been a perfectly reasonable roommate. He only saw her, generally speaking, in the evenings when there was an event. Usually it was her stylist he saw first, coming out of the guest suite looking militant. Annika came shortly after, always looking wary when she approached him. Though she always turned in a circle when he bid her do so, usually by spinning his finger in the air.

I certainly hope my latest outfit meets with your approval, she had said the night before, the mildness of her voice belied by the look in her eyes.

You would be no doubt about it if I did not, he had replied.

She either kept to herself or went out of her way to avoid him. He didn't know which it was, and in truth, did not care. His staff kept him informed of her whereabouts and whatever they did not know, the tabloids were all over. Between the two sources, he knew that Annika had to battle a scrum of cameras every time she left his loft and every time she made her way back up to the Upper East Side to that museum of hers. Where she spent all day doing whatever it was she did, before returning to the loft in time for the evening event they normally had to attend.

If all marriages were so convenient and undemanding, perhaps Ranieri would not be so opposed to the very idea of the institution.

But he knew better. Marriage was not a good bet in his family. Not a one that he could think of in generations had lasted. His grandparents had remained married until their deaths, but had spent the bulk of their years living apart. *The secret to happiness,* his grandfather had told him, laughing uproariously, as prideful as ever.

Ranieri was cursed with the same pride as the rest of them. But he liked to win. Left to his own devices, he never would have married. It was a bad bet. He never would have started something he was reasonably certain would end badly. That had always seemed to him the very opposite of winning.

Annika made him want, a little too badly, to stop caring about things like pride, winning, and everything that wasn't that better-than-vanilla scent.

He thought he might be more furious about that than the dahlia.

Tonight they had no events to attend. He hoped that would mean that Annika had locked herself away, as well she should. If he were her, he would be trembling in fear about what he might do to her here. Far, far away from any outside eyes.

The elevator doors opened up directly into his loft, and he had only taken a few steps inside before he stopped short. And realized that Annika had not taken the wiser course, complete with piteous trembling, as she should have done.

He looked around, trying to make sense of what he saw. But he couldn't. There were...*things* everywhere. Disrupting the clean, stark modern lines he preferred. He moved toward the nearest one, and picked it up, scowling down at it as he held it in his palm.

He was not mistaken.

The infernal woman had covered almost every surface in his home with these...figurines.

His mind did not want to make sense of them.

They were egregious examples of ceramics gone wrong, some of them plump and round, others lean and hooved. But what they all had in common were the colors. Obnoxiously bright pinks. Offensive purples. Golds and pinks.

She had infested his house with bloody *unicorns*.

Still gripping the plump figurine his hand, Ranieri tossed his briefcase aside and stalked off to find her.

She wasn't in the guest room, or barricaded away in the guest bathroom, the way she would have been if she was at all wise. Though he did notice that the guest room, which had never smelled like much of anything, now held that same damned scent that had been haunting him all day.

He was already growling to himself when he climbed the spiral stair to the rooftop garden that transformed the top of the building into an oasis in the middle of this concrete city. His little taste of the Italian countryside, so far from home. Ranieri usually found it soothing.

But there was no possibility of being soothed tonight.

He found her in the bathhouse that contained the hot tub and sauna and small sitting area that he had never used. She was curled up on the sofa with a colorful throw blanket over her legs, a tray of charcuterie on the ottoman, and a thick hardcover book open on her lap.

Annika glanced up when he slammed open the door, but did not otherwise react to his presence.

Then, as he watched, she very calmly picked up a bit of hard salami and cheese and popped them into her mouth, gazing back at him as if he was the unhinged one here.

What Ranieri did not understand was how it was possible that he, widely renowned to have ice water in his veins, actually *felt* unhinged in her presence. But the figurine in his hand was an excellent reminder.

"Do you think you can hide up here?" he demanded, his voice a kind of rasp.

"If I was hiding," she said in the sort of overtly patient voice that suggested that she, for one, felt he was grossly overreacting, "I would be hiding. Instead of sitting here, easily found, and making no attempt whatsoever to spirit myself away."

Ranieri felt coiled tight. Too tight. And once again, he felt that disturbing heaviness in his sex. Once again, he found himself entirely too aware of her.

As a woman.

She was no longer wearing that teal dress. Her hair was down, spilling over her shoulders, and in this little bathhouse, festooned with strands of lights overhead, she seemed to *glow*. It hit him then, like a kick to the chest that she was unquestionably pretty.

How had he never before noticed how *pretty* she was?

She was lounging on that couch, the throw half kicked off, so he could see that she wore a cozy-looking sweater in a copper shade and what he believed were called lounging pants in an understated neutral shade of oatmeal. Both in what looked very much like cashmere.

He should have approved, as it was a serious upgrade from that deplorable T-shirt he'd seen her in that first morning. But what caught his attention instead was that the sweater had ridden up, so that all he could seem to focus on before him was that swathe of skin. A ribbon of delicate ivory, just above her hips.

Ranieri had the nearly ungovernable impulse to set his mouth to that ribbon, then taste every bit of it.

Somehow, he held himself in check. He was not sure how.

When he moved forward, all he did was place the unicorn figurine in the center of her charcuterie platter.

Then he straightened, waiting.

Annika looked at the unicorn and then she lifted her gaze to his.

"My unicorn collection is very important to me," she told him, even though he could see the unholy amusement in her dancing green gaze. "Obviously, anywhere I live, I need all of them around me like magical guardians. It's the only way I can feel at home."

He could have pointed out that he'd spent an inordinate amount of time in the Fifth Avenue apartment she had shared with her father and had never seen even one unicorn. Really, he did not understand why he refrained.

Because she knows full well that you know that she's lying, he scolded himself. *The lying is the point.*

"Today the unwanted delivery of a dahlia and an army of unicorn figurines." He didn't sound like himself. He had the scent of her in his nose again and he was hard and ready, even though this was Annika Schuyler, for God's sake. "What is next, I wonder?"

She had disrupted a meeting, which was sacrosanct to Ranieri and would have gotten anyone who worked for him fired. And yet he had ordered Gregory to keep the damned plant watered. She had absolutely destroyed the sanctuary that was his home, with a rainbow of hideous unicorn tat as far as the eye could see. And still, he did nothing.

Annika very clearly saw her advantage. She sat up, looking entirely too pleased with herself.

"The possibilities are endless," she told him. "After all, as you pointed out to me before, I'm already known to be a disaster. Why not an emotional disaster? I know you care about very little as much as you care about your reputation. And it occurred to me that I don't have a reputation."

"Oh, you do. Be assured of that."

She only laughed. "I don't have a reputation I care about. That's the difference. So really, Ranieri. The sky's the limit."

He scowled at her, and she laughed.

She laughed and she kept right on laughing. She laughed so much that the offensively bright unicorn before her seemed to laugh with her. The lights were too bright, and she was too pretty, and his sex pulsed as if he'd been some kind of monk—possibly for years—and then he was moving.

Without thought, when he never acted without thinking it through.

Never—but then he was reaching down and wrapping his hands around the tops of her arms.

And then he thought a lot about the way she stopped laughing, her green eyes going wide, and that sensual mouth of hers dropping open. Especially when she made the sweetest little sound.

Ranieri lifted her up, letting the throw fall aside and the book she'd been reading crash to the floor.

He hauled her up and then, as if he'd been longing to do nothing else for the whole of his existence, Ranieri—who had never been carried away by passion in his life—slammed his mouth to Annika's at last.

And drank her in, deep.

CHAPTER FIVE

SHE WASN'T PREPARED.

It was the only thought that scrolled through her head, because everything else was him.

Ranieri. The press of his lips, the rough heat of his tongue.

She felt shivery and strange. And swollen with a new heat, because he tasted forbidden, somehow beautiful, and she could feel him everywhere.

Every time his tongue touched hers, she could feel an answering wildfire ignite between her legs. She felt slippery, outside herself, and yet more *in* herself than ever before, because she could feel…*everything.*

Annika was suddenly, unbearably *aware* of her breasts. They felt too large, too tender, and her nipples ached. He shifted so that she was pressed against him and there was something about the pressure that made her want to squirm wildly. But not to get away.

He kissed her the way he did everything. Fully. Masterfully.

She did not have to be an expert in kissing to know that he had perfected the form. It was something about his ferocity. It translated all too well to this. All that grimness, all that starkness, all the maddening things about this man were distilled into the way his tongue slid against hers. The way he angled his head so he could go deeper, so he could take more of her, so that the blistering heat of this could wash over her, changing her.

As if wanting him, tasting him, made her new.

Her hands dug into his shoulders, and she could hardly sift through all the new information she was taking on board. All the immediate, tactile knowledge of too many things she had previously not allowed herself to consider.

How those muscles of his felt to the touch, for example. What it was like to have her breasts flattened against the wall of his chest. How it felt to let her hands discover how hot his skin was, there in that complicated dance of smooth muscle between his neck, his shoulders, and his arms.

She wanted to kiss him forever.

It was as if he heard that thought, because he made a low noise—she could taste it, and more, she could feel it *inside her*—and set her aside.

Annika staggered back, catching herself before

she collapsed back down on the sofa. And not because he let go of her harshly. Or pushed her. But because her legs no longer seemed to function the way they had only moments before.

Or maybe it hadn't been moments. Maybe he'd been kissing her for a lifetime.

She could hear her own breath between them, harsh and loud.

Yet what astonished her was that she could hear his breath, too.

And maybe on some level she imagined his kiss was a punishment. For her version of the unicorn invasion. It was a punishment she couldn't quite decide if she'd loved or not, because she was fairly certain it had broken something in her—

But he was breathing heavily, too.

As if he was just as affected as she was here.

And for a moment there was only the sound of their breath, and all that jangly, wild, too-hot sensation spinning around between them.

Everything is different now.

The words echoed in Annika's head, but she shoved them aside because she didn't want that to be true. Yet what she wanted didn't seem to matter when the way his gaze raked over her was new. She could see the heat in it. And more, she could see some kind of echo of that kiss they'd shared.

The passion between them. She could feel all that gold as if it was inside her.

As if it swirled around and around, centering itself in all the places she ached the most.

"I will expect to find every last one of those unicorns removed," he gritted out at her.

But he didn't sound like...*him*. Or not like any version of him she'd heard before. His voice was too rough. An edgy velvet that made her nipples nearly hurt.

"I expect to wake up every day and find myself the Queen of England," Annika replied, and she supposed she didn't sound any better. His eyes seemed to darken when he heard her. She promptly cleared her throat. "It looks like neither one of us is going to get what we want."

"On the contrary."

And Annika had been looking at Ranieri Furlan for years. She had cataloged him as if he were an artifact in her museum. She'd made no secret of the fact that she'd studied him thoroughly. And still, it was as if she'd never seen him before tonight.

Because now she knew how he tasted.

Now she knew what it was like to have passion punch through her in an instant, igniting...everything.

Now she knew.

"What a surprise you would find a way to be

contrary in all things," she said, fighting hard to make herself sound dry and amused, because surely that was safer than all this *aching*.

"I intend to get exactly what I want, Annika," he said, his voice clipped. "I always do. You would do well to remember that."

And she wanted to offer some smart remark in return. Something quippy at the very least. She wanted to stand her ground and show that she was tougher than him.

But she didn't feel tough at the moment. She felt…slippery. Everywhere. And the gold of his eyes was like a molten hot liquid and she was filled with it. Near to bursting, she was very much afraid.

Worse, she suspected he knew it.

His mouth moved into something just this side of grim, but it was all the more sensual because she knew how deliciously hard that mouth felt against her lips. And, God help her, she would have done almost anything for more just then.

When he turned and slammed his way out of the bathhouse, she told herself that she should have been grateful.

She really should have been.

But gratitude didn't really top her list as she stayed there, sinking down onto the couch again, her fingers to her lips. Even though she pressed hard, to remind herself.

Or maybe to relive it.

Annika stayed there well into the night, her body still wild and her head still spinning.

She expected Ranieri to greet her the following morning with more grim demands, or lists of tasks he wanted her to perform, but he was nowhere to be found. She found the staff guiltily removing the last of the unicorn figurines from the common areas, though they had left several in her room. As if they were concerned that she really might love them as much as she'd said she did.

Or as if he was concerned.

But she couldn't let herself think things like that. It made everything inside her feel...delicate. Instead, she decided to take the absence of the figurines as a sign she needed to come up with something better to break him.

Because surely that was what she'd seen in him last night. That he was *that close* to breaking. And if he broke, she won.

Annika assured herself, repeatedly, that she wanted that more than anything.

A few nights later, she thought she had her chance.

Fall had come in hard over the past few days, with blustery weather and the kind of wind that got into her bones. Marissa dressed her for the night's benefit gala, going for a gown in a deep, lustrous jewel-toned velvet, accessorizing everything with the soft gleam of rose gold.

"We'll stay away from extraneous jewels," the stylist told her briskly. "Your engagement is so new and your wedding is so soon. Best to highlight the ring. It's all anyone is looking at anyway."

And because Ranieri wasn't waiting for her out in the loft's main living space the way he normally was when she was finally ready, Annika had the opportunity to study that ring herself.

It was an eyesore, there was no getting around it, but it was also outrageously beautiful. And oddly enough, it sat easily on her hand. She wanted to complain about it. She wanted to pretend it dragged her hand down and was giving her some kind of ostentation-caused arthritis, but it wasn't. When she studied the ring in the light, it was hard to pretend she didn't find herself seduced by it. She gazed into it and disappeared there, as one facet after the next seemed to draw her deep into the heart of the stone—

"Everyone falls under the spell of that ring eventually," came Ranieri's dark, forbidding voice. "Even you, it seems. Careful, Annika. It might well enchant you."

She looked up to find him wearing formal attire, which instantly made her mouth go dry. Dressed all in black, his gold eyes seemed to glow. With malice, she tried to tell herself. Or maybe it was mockery. Whatever it was, it seemed to hum inside her.

Because she had the terrible suspicion that the only enchantment around here was him.

"I was just wondering how many lives could have been made better for the price of this ring," she blurted out, because she had to say something and his golden gaze was scalding her. She could feel it there between her legs, where she was already too soft and too hot.

"You are known to be one of the foremost champions of sustainability," he replied, his tone deeply sardonic. She bristled, but he didn't wait for her to shoot something back at him. "That is, naturally, why I didn't buy you a new ring. I thought you would appreciate that it is an heirloom. I thought that was your stock-in-trade?"

He didn't wait for her to respond to that, either. He nodded off to the side and staff appeared at once to present them with coats to ward off the brooding autumn night outside.

It took her the whole way down in the elevator, fuming, to remind herself that she only had a few days left before the wedding. There had to be a way to get him to break this off before it got that far. She hoped that tonight's gala would provide her with the perfect opportunity to nudge him in that direction.

Annika didn't necessarily enjoy making a fool

out of herself. But since she managed to do it all the time without meaning to, why not do it on purpose? She daydreamed about simply…having her life back. Endless, easy days in the museum. Retreating into her apartment. The odd meal out with friends without the assault of flashing cameras everywhere she turned.

It sounded lovely, that life she'd lost.

Out in front of his building, Ranieri helped her into the car, then climbed in after her. And then there they sat, cocooned together in the warm, plush darkness.

She could feel her pulse take her over, as if she was about to have a heart attack. Annika thought that sounded like a lovely reprieve, given what was actually happening to her.

"It was never my intention to remain faithful to a bride I did not choose for myself and, indeed, never would have chosen at all," Ranieri announced.

Almost conversationally.

And it was the oddest thing. Annika had given absolutely no thought to fidelity in this relationship at all. Mostly because she didn't accept that they were in a relationship, that kiss notwithstanding. And as much as she might have thought, in a gauzy sort of fashion, that should she ever find herself married she would require an appropriate level of faithfulness…she still couldn't quite believe she was going to have to marry this man.

Is the problem that you have to *marry him?* a voice inside her asked, too knowingly. *Or that there is no small part of you that thinks, just maybe, it wouldn't be the worst thing in the world?*

She shoved that thought away, feeling betrayed. By herself.

All of that raced through her head in the wake of his statement.

Followed by a searing burst of outrage that he had thought about all of those things himself and had decided that he would stray.

She couldn't make sense of it.

"Thank you so much for informing me," she murmured. Stiffly.

"I'm out of the habit of engaging sexually with women of your…" He turned his head and she was speared, suddenly, by all that gold.

"Education?" she supplied. A bit crisply. "Self-confidence? Disinterest in you?"

"But now I think perhaps that was unduly hasty."

And once again, she found her throat had gone bone-dry.

"I would be perfectly happy if you would remain faithless," she told him, even though something in her turned over in dismay as the words came out of her mouth. "That you pride yourself on being the master of all things yet would find it impossible to keep your wedding vows seems emblematic of you as a person, Ranieri. I wouldn't want that ruined."

His mouth curved slightly, acknowledging the jab. "I always keep my promises," he told her. "I would have made it clear to you what I was and was not promising. I would not have snuck around, though any dalliances would never have been something you would need to confront during the course of our union. But the truth is, Annika, I think perhaps that you can meet my needs after all."

"Your *needs*," she repeated.

But she could hardly hear herself speak. Her pulse was a mad roar in her head. And a danger everywhere else.

And as if he knew it, Ranieri smiled, that little crook in the corner of his mouth. And then, making her pulse go wild inside her, he reached over and took her chin between his thumb and two fingers.

All he did was tilt her head toward him. But it felt to her like a clamp of impossible heat, not merely localized to her chin, but taking over the rest of her.

She couldn't understand it.

But understanding did not appear to be required, not when he was holding her like that, so that the two of them were practically huddled together there in the back seat.

Close enough that if he'd wanted to, he could have taken her mouth once more, and pleased them both—

Stop that, she snapped at herself. *This is not about pleasure. You're supposed to be coming up with ways to shake this man.*

Oddly, none came to mind.

"As in many arenas," he said after a moment, that same gold light so hot inside her it nearly hurt, "I'm drawn to quality. But I also have certain requirements when it comes to quantity."

"Are you… Are you talking about sex?"

And maybe the racket in her pulse was shorting out her brain, because she could have sworn she saw a different expression in those golden eyes of his then. It spread across his face. He looked very nearly…amused?

She didn't dare think the word *affectionate.*

"I see no reason why our marriage of convenience cannot be even more convenient, for us both," he said as if he was simply making a rational observation. As if he wasn't talking about sex— and with his hand on her. "It was obvious that there was some chemistry here the other night. As much as I wish to disbelieve it, I find I cannot deny it."

Her heart was knocking much too hard against her ribs, and she was finding it difficult to sit still.

"It's the compliments, really," she managed to say. She tugged her chin back to break his grasp—

but he didn't let go. Just for a moment. Just to show her that he could have held her fast if he'd wanted to. But then he released her, and she felt a rush of something she told herself sternly was relief. Even if it felt a whole lot more like regret. "They go straight to my head. It's overwhelming, Ranieri. It's almost as if they might be fake, you shower them upon me with such abandon."

"Because you have always been such a particular fan of mine?" He shook his head, but his mouth was still crooked in that corner. "But then, it will not be the first time in history that enemies become lovers, will it?"

He was talking as if it was all a foregone conclusion and she felt the heat of that assumption as if she'd poured molten gold all over her. She could feel it at the back of her eyes. She could feel it carving its way deep into the center of her, that place where she was hungriest.

More hungry than she had ever been before—but she didn't want to focus on that. It was too dangerous. That was clear to her, no matter how new and sharp and breathtaking that hunger was.

"I think you're overlooking an important point here," she told him, trying to sound stern and only coming off a bit wispy. She cleared her throat, but that only made his eyes gleam the brighter. "I have no desire to… Um. Consummate this relationship."

"Do you not?"

"I do not. I *certainly* do not."

But she knew they could both hear that under-current of longing in her voice.

"We will see." Ranieri settled back against his seat as if it was all the same to him, this casual talk of sexual needs and *lovers*. "It will be difficult otherwise. Not to find a willing woman, you understand. But to find the sort of regularity I prefer while making certain that the woman in question does not come away with any ideas about what I might offer her. That is always the most difficult part."

"Yes, I'm certain it's very hard to be you," she managed to say.

What she was thinking about instead was regular sex. Did he mean daily? Nightly? More than that?

Contemplating the possibilities made her feel light-headed.

She was still feeling dizzy when they arrived at the gala. So dizzy and gold-drunk as they stepped onto the red carpet to face the gauntlet of reporters that she almost let Ranieri hurry her along inside. She almost passed up this opportunity.

Because she was too busy thinking about sex, multiple times a day, with this man and his *needs*.

But then she remembered that she didn't want any part of that. That what she wanted was her very own, perfectly happy life of artifacts and old trinkets and beautiful pieces of art. And that wasn't going to happen unless she *did something*.

She looked up at Ranieri as he took her arm and then she took a deep, full breath, because she fully intended to project the nickname he hated so loudly that it bounced up and down the entire island of Manhattan.

That breath gave her away.

Because Ranieri tugged her to him, then gripped her waist. He pulled her close, as if they were dancing.

And then suddenly, before she knew what was happening, he was tilting her down over his arm in a parody of a grand dip.

"What on earth…?" she began.

"This is romantic," he growled, not even bothering to smile, his mouth close to hers. "Ask anyone."

Then he kissed her again, right there, while the flashbulbs put on a light show.

A kiss so thorough that it made her too giddy to mind. And when he finally set her upright again, inclined his head toward the paparazzi, and ushered her into the gala, she had completely forgotten that she'd intended to call him out to the tabloids as *Ranieri Berry* in the first place.

The following morning, she saw that picture—that kiss—plastered everywhere. And what she'd taken as a grim, hard expression on his face looked like... intensity. Passion. An almost unendurable need.

While she looked...

It made that shivering thing inside her go wild to look at herself. Because she looked absolutely transported.

Very much like a woman who was marrying the love of her life in a matter of days.

It's possible, that same voice inside her chimed in, clearly not impressed with any sense of betrayal she might feel, *that this has all been you protesting a bit too much. Isn't it?*

And she tried her best to nip this all in the bud, truly she did, because she was all too aware of the truth of things. No matter how he tasted.

Every time they went anywhere together, she tried again.

But Ranieri cut her off with a kiss here, a deeper kiss there. Always in front of people. Always in front of cameras. Because any venue that she could try to use to embarrass him was the same sort of situation that he could turn against her.

Which he did.

Proving to all the world that the great passion between them was real, after all.

Maybe proving it to you, too, came that voice, inevitably.

Damn him.

And that was how she woke up on the morning of her wedding day, surely and totally doomed, because she hadn't made any headway at all in getting him to call this off.

But as she looked at the set of photographs splashed across the usual papers from the night before—because they hadn't bothered with a re-hearsal dinner when there was an art show to attend and no rehearsal necessary for a forced travesty—she didn't see a woman who was one short, fitful sleep away from being married off to appease her late father.

Annika saw herself looking bright and flushed.

She looked like she was well and truly his.

And though she should have been distraught today, *doomed* was not how she felt at all.

CHAPTER SIX

THE WEDDING WENT precisely as Ranieri had planned.

It was true that the Schuyler House museum baffled him. There it sat on a side street on Upper East Side, lost, to his mind, between the flashier museums that littered the area. The Metropolitan. The Guggenheim. The Frick.

But there was no denying that using Schuyler House leant this wedding of his a certain extra glow.

Even the weather dared not defy him. It was a spectacular afternoon. The deep blue of the sky was a color only possible here in the fall, and yet this first Saturday in October was neither chilly nor overly warm. As if the skies above approved of the outdoor venue he had chosen.

The house was built in that old Gilded Age style, and rather than rearrange the museum—and contend with Annika's potential reaction to that—Ranieri had decided that the back courtyard was more appropriate. He had found the best event planners the city, offered them enough money to make this last-minute high society wedding a prospect too appealing to turn down, and today he found himself pleased with the results.

Perhaps he was particular. But *particular* got results.

He had several fortunes to prove it.

Ranieri stood at the head of the aisle the event planners had constructed there in the walled stone courtyard. He waited for his bride while a select number of the world's and New York City's wealthiest—as well as Annika's close friends—filled the few rows of chairs. And when Annika finally appeared, a single violin began to play.

She caught his gaze and stood there a moment, and he wondered—not quite idly—if she might attempt to play one of her tricks here. But instead, she gripped the bouquet she held before her a little tighter and then she started down the wide stone steps at the back of the old house.

And then she headed straight for him.

Ranieri had planned every part of this wedding. Including the dress she wore now, because he'd known that its elegant sweep would highlight her beauty perfectly. He was pleased to see it did. She looked graceful and ethereal, a vision in white.

He had slowly come to terms with the reality

of Annika over the past few weeks. Perhaps it was simply that once he'd kissed her, all the blinders he'd kept firmly in place for years had come crashing down.

Annika was a beautiful woman. Full stop. What she was not, he had found, was overly concerned with maintaining and showing off that beauty. He doubted she thought much about it at all. Just as she did not care overmuch about fashion the way everyone did—including him—because it was considered a calling card in these circles.

She had never been interested in calling cards. If she was, she would not have secreted herself away in this funny old museum.

And Ranieri knew this: if she had truly been as embarrassing and awkward as she and everyone around her pretended, she would not have inspired the kind of snide commentary that forever followed in her wake. That sort of thing only came about when jealousy was involved.

It made sense. A beautiful woman so unselfconscious could only be considered a threat to some.

Not that this explained his long-term aversion to her and what he liked to think of as her bedraggled state. Kissing her had brought other memories back, too. He could recall his first introduction to her. She'd been standing there in the stunning foyer of her apartment, beneath the Baccarat chandelier with her father, and he had taken a quick initial impression of her. He'd seen the long, silky hair. Her lovely oval of a face. An hourglass figure in a lovely dress. He'd noticed, because of course he noticed, how pretty she was—

And in the next moment she had been introduced to him as Bennett Schuyler's daughter and he had shut all of that off. So completely that it was as if he hadn't truly seen her again until now.

But it made sense to him why her sartorial choices had always irritated him so deeply. Why he had only been able to see the careless hair, the oddball choices of dress. If asked, he would have banged on about the stain upon the Schuyler name, which affected him personally in his position. He often had, at length.

Now he rather thought the truth of it was, deep down, that he'd always known exactly how pretty she was. And it offended him, connoisseur of all things beautiful, that her loveliness was obscured. When all it would take was a little work on her part to showcase it.

Today, he'd done the showcasing himself.

And he had done it well.

What he hadn't been prepared for was the punch to the gut he felt when he laid eyes on her for the first time in the dress he'd picked out for her, walking toward him as if she'd chosen this.

As if she'd chosen him.

It was as if that violin was scratching out the bridal march inside him.

Annika had opted to walk down the aisle herself. And though Ranieri knew she'd done it because she thought that somehow made what was happening less real, he thought she'd miscalculated. It didn't make her look removed from the proceedings, but the opposite. She could not have made her father more present here in any other way.

All anyone could possibly see as she walked was his absence. The afternoon shadows almost seemed to make it possible to imagine him walking proudly beside her as she made it down the aisle and faced Ranieri at last.

And he felt everything far too keenly, though he told himself it was the sweetness of his victory here, nothing more.

He reminded himself of that victory when she took his hands. When he said his vows and her green eyes darkened. When she repeated them, her voice gone ever so slightly scratchy on those old words that he knew she would say did not apply to them.

Love. Honor. Cherish.

Then it was done, so Ranieri hooked a hand around her neck and pulled her close to kiss her. Once more for a crowd.

They were getting good at it, this kissing thing. He had staved off God only knew how many humiliations this way, and now was done. The marriage her father had demanded, sealed with a kiss.

Now if either one of them wanted to walk away, it would take a divorce.

The reception kicked into gear as they walked back down the aisle and posed for a few pictures, because not doing so would look strange. When the photographer had snapped what must have been hundreds of shots, Annika murmured something about tending to the guests, and excused herself.

Ran away from him, more like, but Ranieri could allow it. There was nowhere for her to go, after all. He did his own rounds of the party, checking in with the usual heavy hitters he always found himself talking to at parties like this. He liked that the caterers Annika had recommended were deft and seemed functionally psychic, replacing a drink the very moment a guest noticed it was empty. Or producing a plate of appetizers to choose from at the very moment someone *almost* felt hungry.

He was tempted to imagine that if they wished, the two of them could do well together. Stuck as they were with each other for the year. Today, it seemed less a bitter fate than before.

The events coordinator oversaw the removal of all the chairs from the ceremony and swiftly set up the single long table down the length of the courtyard as the sun began to set. The courtyard was lit all around with lanterns, a bright glow against the October evening, with heat lamps placed every few feet to keep the warmth of the day. Schuyler House stood there before them, its old walls surrounded them, and Ranieri almost thought he understood Annika's connection to the place now. It was beautiful, in its way. A slice of old New York and, having grown up in so many old places himself, Ranieri felt drawn to it.

When really, he should've been basking in his triumph. His complete and utter victory, despite much provocation from Annika herself. Despite the pink monstrosity that was still overtaking his desk and *unicorn figurines*.

But in truth, all he could think about was the honeymoon. About getting away from all these *people* at last and taking her somewhere that there would be no eyes on her at all, save his.

The violinist was joined by three other musicians to form a proper string quartet, and they played classical standards as the party was called to dinner. Ranieri wasn't hungry. Not for food. But what he liked was that it gave him a good excuse to do what he wanted to do anyway. He found his way to his bride's side, intending to take her hand and tug her away from the conversation she was hav-

ing with the group of women he knew were the college friends she sometimes spoke of. Not to him,
but to the staff when she thought he wasn't paying
attention.

She had not yet learned that he always paid attention.

"There you are," he said as he came up beside
her. As if he might have lost track of her in the small
crowd. Or ever.

Then he found himself smiling slightly as her
friends all turned the same sort of steely, assess-
ing looks upon him.

"Do you not have a family?" one of them asked.
"Is that why none of them are here?"

"Or are you estranged from your family?" asked
another.

His brand-new wife frowned at her friends, but
her smile was apologetic when she aimed it at him.
"They're very nosy and wholly ungovernable," she
told him. "I told them to leave it alone, but you see
how well that went."

"We can't be contained," said the third friend
with a shrug. "But it is interesting…" She lingered
over that word as if it was the clue they'd all been
looking for, and perhaps it was "…that your side
of the aisle was all business associates, isn't it?"

Ranieri acknowledged her with the barest lift

of his brow. "I admire this support for your friend. But I must steal her away."

And then, he steered Annika away with him, giving her no choice but to follow him—unless she wished to make a scene. He rather thought her appetite for scenes had diminished these past few days. Maybe it was because she viewed the wedding as a setback, having failed to make him call it off. Or possibly it was because he kept responding to each attempt on her part to make a scene with a kiss.

Either way, though he braced himself for her to struggle with him now, she didn't.

He led her over to the center of the long table and seated her, then took the chair beside her. All around them, the guests filled in the empty seats, and then the caterers outdid themselves as they began to serve the simple, but exquisitely prepared meal that Ranieri had chosen.

Yet he could barely taste it.

Beside him, Annika only picked at the food on her plate. And Ranieri almost laughed, because to all appearances, it must have looked as if they were consumed with the sort of wedding nerves normally reserved for people in love. That or virgins, tremulously expecting the unknown on their wedding night.

"If you wish to ask me questions about my personal life, you should simply ask," he said, sitting back in his seat and looping his arm on the back of her chair, because he could. Because she was his wife. And possibly also because she didn't sit up straight to get away from him, so his fingers could graze the delicate strap of her dress, the tempting line of her shoulder blade.

"I don't know what makes you think I have the faintest interest in your personal life," she said, but she didn't say such things the way she had at first. Her voice was warm. And the look she shot him was green and bright.

"It must be your friends, then, who are so interested. Such that they feel it reasonable to interrogate me at my own wedding."

Annika shifted around in her seat to look at him then. And it should not have surprised him as much as it did, the way the rest of the reception seemed to fall away. As if it was only the two of them out here in the Manhattan night.

He would have sworn they were entirely alone.

"I'm the very last of my family. And there's not a lot I wouldn't do to bring them back, if I could." Annika glanced away briefly, her eyes moving over the museum and then returning to him. Almost shyly, he thought, or perhaps that was a trick of the lantern light. "It's not really a surprise that I've chosen to spend my life immersed in all this family history. It's the closest I can get to the real thing."

Ranieri felt very nearly…unsettled, and that was a new sensation. He had to fight the urge to rub his free hand over his chest.

"This seems unduly introspective," he said, but softly. Very softly, and not, for once, because he wished to score any points. "But it is not surprising. Weddings can be very emotional."

He would not have thought so, previously. They had always been networking opportunities to him. But in this moment of sudden, bracing honesty, here in this private little bubble between them despite the fact they were surrounded on all sides, he found it was easy to admit it.

Alarmingly easy, as though it took nothing from him. He had to consider that its own sort of win, he supposed.

"Everything happened so fast," Annika told him, almost gravely. "It wasn't until I walked down the aisle that it really hit me. My father isn't here. I actually got married without him."

Her green eyes were too bright, for a moment. She lowered her gaze. And he had to fight not to reach over and pull her to him. He didn't know why it occurred to him to try. When had he last offered anyone comfort? But this was Annika.

He allowed his hand to move, rising until he could wrap his palm over the nape of her neck. It wasn't enough, he felt certain. But it was something.

She looked at him again and took a steadying sort of breath, and he wasn't sure if the warmth he felt in his hand was hers or his. Perhaps it was both of theirs.

"I think I've decided to be grateful that I didn't have to anticipate the loss," she said in the same grave tone. "I didn't spend years having to imagine walking down a wedding aisle without him. It happened so fast that it's already done."

"I'm delighted that could be a part of this...expediency."

That should have come out sardonic. Hadn't he meant it to? But instead, he said it with the same weight and gravity she had used.

And more astounding, Ranieri found he meant it.

Her gaze rose to meet his again and they were not kissing. Not now. Yet somehow, that was what this moment felt like anyway. There was heat, intensity. There was that breathlessness. He wasn't sure that he had ever felt connected like this to anyone.

The closest he had ever come had been when he'd been deep inside a woman, and he would not compare the experiences. This felt...sacred.

It occurred to him to pay attention to where he was. The clink of the glasses around them, the sparkling conversations. The eyes on them, everywhere, even as Annika quietly took him apart.

He assured himself that all of this was about sex. Sex and the year ahead, that was all.

That was all it ever could be.

As the dinner wore on, Annika lost that hint of melancholy. Or emotion, of whatever stripe. She got up from her seat and walked around the table, talking to whoever stopped her, and Ranieri learned some more things about her then. That she was not, perhaps, as awkward as she always appeared at galas and the like. That here, with her friends nearby and only a few close business associates to contend with, she bloomed.

He wasn't sure how it had never occurred to him that the secret of Annika Schuyler was simply that she was shy. Ranieri tried to tell himself that she was putting on an act here the same way she did elsewhere, but he couldn't quite make himself believe it. He'd seen the genuine emotion in her gaze. More than that, he had tasted her now.

And a person could fake a great many things, but a kiss was not one of them.

Not the way Annika kissed him, as if she might die if she stopped.

Act or not, the result was the same. She had invited her friends. He had made strategic choices for the guest list and he knew full well that all of them would tell tales about Annika Schuyler Furlan's easy, elegant hospitality for years to come.

He would have set about congratulating himself, but he had far more pressing things on his mind.

Like the marital relations she had seemed so shocked to discover he wanted.

Ranieri might have been shocked too, but he wanted her too badly. And while he had never been led around by the hardest part of him in his life, he hadn't been married before, either. All bets appeared well and truly off.

After dinner was done, the string quartet began to play dancing music. Ranieri gritted his teeth and got to it.

Because that was the most expedient way to fast-forward to the part he was actually interested in. He strode over to Annika, involved in another deep discussion with her college cohort, and drew her away once more.

This time without an interrogation.

"That was rude," she told him, looking over her shoulder at her friends.

"This is not a reunion, *amore*," he told her, loud enough that her friends were not the only ones who could hear the endearment he used. "You are the bride. You have certain duties, and one of them, I am afraid, is that you must dance with your husband."

He was suddenly overtly aware of the platinum band on his finger. And the slender, matching band

Annika now wore, because she hadn't wanted more diamonds. She had felt the single one she wore was more than enough. She had said as much, repeatedly, waving his family heirloom around as if she would have liked it if it flew off and shattered the nearest window.

Ranieri drew her out into the middle of the courtyard that been set aside as a dance floor, and pulled her into his arms at last. Where she fit too well and he was a little too invested in that.

He told himself that, too, was about sex.

The truth was he couldn't recall the last time he had been required to wait.

The strings played, singing out an ancient song of love, and he whirled her around, again and again.

And while the music played, Ranieri did not think of winning or losing. He did not calculate the advantages here or plot out his next move. He only held her in his arms, this woman who had become his wife, gazed down at her, and lost himself in all that marvelous green.

Grave again, as if she could see the deepest parts of him. The things no one ever saw.

Finally, when the dancing was done, he drew her with him as he climbed the steps of the museum.

"Are you planning to make a speech?" she asked as they went. "What a good host you are, Ranieri. I doubt anyone saw that coming."

He liked that dry little bit of teasing in her voice. It made him feel like himself again. It chased away all the unexpected weight of this odd emotion he couldn't seem to dispel.

"Only in a manner of speaking," he told her. "My ferocious reputation will remain spotless, I promise you."

And then, while their assembled guests watched and applauded—or in the case of her friends, frowned—he bent slightly, then swept her into his arms. Ranieri held her there for a moment, so the whole of the wedding reception could see them. So the photographers could be certain to take the last picture for some time.

Then he turned without another word and bore her into the museum.

Ranieri did not put her down. He carried her straight through the museum, then out the front door, and deposited her in his waiting car.

"I think this counts as a kidnapping," she said, but she did not sound unduly concerned at the prospect.

"I would not be surprised to discover that many a honeymoon started off the same way," he replied, unrepentantly.

And then, finally, Ranieri kissed her the way he wanted to.

He feasted on her as the car pulled away from

the curb, carrying them off to the jet that waited for them in a private airfield.

She surged against him, tasting of the same hunger that burned so hot and wild within him. He kissed her and he kissed her, and this time, they were safely ensconced in the back of a moving car. There were no watching eyes. No cameras.

No acts to perform.

He could indulge himself.

And so, at last, that was what he did.

Ranieri succumbed to the temptation of her mouth, angling his head as he took the kiss deeper. And while he was at it, he let his hands explore the glory of that figure of hers she had so long kept concealed.

He wanted to take that as some kind of evidence of her perfidy, even now, but he couldn't get past the notion of her shyness. Her disinterest in the games so many in her set played.

And the possibility that it had never occurred to her that her figure was a gift.

One he did not intend to share.

He bent his head to press his mouth to the graceful line of her neck, then followed it down. He lavished attention on the sweet, rounded mounds that rose above the bodice of her gown.

But he wanted more. He wanted some proof that

he was not alone in this wanting. This need that had taken him over, little as he wished to admit it.

He pulled her voluminous skirts up with him, still kissing her. And he reveled in every noise she made. Because she sounded greedy and half-mad, just as he felt.

And because he could taste the sounds she made, and that made him even harder.

He found the garter she wore, and he moved his fingers up higher. Then still higher, until he found the soft heat of her at last.

"Ranieri…" she whispered brokenly.

But her hips rose as she said his name. And she opened herself beneath his hands, giving herself over to him that easily.

As if this was no surrender, but an invitation.

He traced the shape of her, learning the soft, hot contours of her femininity. The scent of her was wilder now, but still that same sweetness that was only hers. And only when she was shuddering in his arms, her head thrown back and her back arched as if offering herself to him on the altar of his choosing, did he test the tight clasp of her heat.

Then, following an urge that felt like a drumbeat within him, he tested her heat with one finger, then another. She sighed, and opened herself even farther as he set a slow, unhurried pace, twisting his hand around to let his thumb press hard against the center of her need.

Now, finally, she was his.

Ranieri gazed down at her, her face flushed, her head thrown back, the very picture of grace and greed.

He had never wanted a woman more.

In point of fact, he could no longer recall if any other women existed.

After only a few thrusts, Annika bucked all around him, flooding his hands with her sweet heat.

Ranieri forced himself to sit back. He rearranged her skirts, and found himself smiling as he pulled her up from where she'd gone limp against the seat, arranging her so that she looked a proper bride and not the debauched creature he'd made her.

That she was both of those things, and both were his, pleased him deeply.

It took her some time to open her eyes and when she did, the green of her eyes seemed to pierce him straight through.

"But… Don't you want to…?"

"Amore," he said with a certain intensity, and did not choose to ask himself why he was using that particular endearment when there was no one but her to hear it, "you are a Furlan now. And I am taking you to my ancestral home, such as it is. Where I will sample you as is only good and proper and

civilized, in an actual bed. Not in the back of a car as if we are nothing but overwrought teenagers."

If she didn't matter to you, you wouldn't bother to wait, a voice inside him whispered.

He ignored it.

Annika stared at him for a long moment. Then a smile took over her face. And this was not the kind of smile he'd grown used to from her. This one seemed to crack her wide open, until all he could see was sunlight, and no matter that outside the car the October night was dark and deep.

"Yes, dear," she said, almost diffidently, and then her smile widened. "Isn't that the appropriate, sub-servient mode of address? Is that what we're look-ing for here?"

And Ranieri had to shift on the seat before he forgot his good intentions and had her here and now—

But he was taking her home. And he would wait until he got her there, or really, he could count him-self no better than animal. Something he was cer-tain he would have to remind himself of during the flight ahead of them.

If she didn't matter to you...

Ranieri took her hand and played with his grand-mother's ring, sitting so snugly on her finger. "I'm glad you're taking your wifely duties so seriously,

Annika," he said, and found himself smiling again at her laughter. "See that it continues."

Then he allowed himself one more kiss.

But only the one.

CHAPTER SEVEN

To Annika's tremendous disappointment, Ranieri meant what he said.

And he could not be moved.

There was that lovely interlude in the car, and that was it. They boarded the jet waiting for them and he ushered her to one of the rooms on the plane, gruffly suggesting that she take the opportunity to change out of her wedding gown. She might have wanted to argue about that, or suggest he stay with her in the stateroom, but Marissa appeared and bustled into the room with her. Because, it occurred to her only after Ranieri left her there, she could not get out of her wedding gown on her own. It had taken a handful of attendants to get her into it earlier.

And when she was finally changed and comfortably ensconced in the sort of lounging clothing that Marissa approved of—all cashmere and merino wool, which were not exactly a hardship to wear, though she hated to admit it—she wandered out into the main part of the plane to see if she could find Ranieri again.

He wasn't hard to locate. He was in his own stateroom but he was seated at a desk with his laptop open and his briefcase beside him, talking gruffly in what sounded like German. Annika supposed she could have disrupted whatever meeting he was conducting on his wedding day, but she didn't. She was still floating on the remains of the day they'd had—and what had gone on in the back of that limousine.

She was still flashing too hot, thinking about *his hand.*

How had she let it happen?

But she knew the answer to that. They had been alone as they had not been since that kiss up on his roof. And all the kisses in between, parceled out to the paparazzi as little punishments for her attempts to shame him, had stoked a greedy, breathless fire within her. The wedding had made it worse. Walking down that aisle to him. Dancing with him.

Being swept up in his arms and carried off.

There with Schuyler House looking on like the benevolent relatives she missed so dearly.

She had lost herself. There was no other way to describe it. And she should have been barricading herself away from him now, but she couldn't quite get there. She didn't *want* to get there.

Because there was that fire in her and there had been his *hand*, and now she no longer wanted to deny it. To fight it with dahlias and unicorns and nicknames. Now she wanted to know where it went.

She wanted to chase that fire, not run away from it.

He had talked about needs. It turned out she had some, too. Why shouldn't they both get what they wanted out of this situation? She felt wildly sophisticated as she thought that—like the woman she looked like in the mirror now, the woman he dressed her to be these days. Theirs was a temporary arrangement, so why not enjoy it?

If he could do it, why couldn't she?

Why not *choose* to burn?

All she had to do was take care of her heart, she thought, as it beat too hard. Much too hard, there in her chest. She just needed to make sure this all stayed sophisticated. And that she didn't get too... silly about this. About him. Because these were games people played all the time, and that meant she could, too. She was sure she could, no matter how dangerously attractive he was.

That in mind, Annika made her way back to her room and, without meaning to, curled up beneath the blanket on the bed and fell asleep.

Something she was only aware of when she woke up as the plane began its descent.

This time, when she walked out into the main cabin, Ranieri beckoned her into the seat beside him. And maybe she should have worried about how eager she was to take the place he offered her. Maybe she should have questioned why it was that the wedding she hadn't even wanted had turned her around this much. It was only a wedding, after all. Not even one she'd had a hand in planning. She knew it was practically fashionable these days to have any number of weddings, follow them up with divorces, and treat it all like a series of amusing parties.

But Annika wasn't that woman. She wasn't sure, as she sat there next to Ranieri feeling a little bit silly and entirely too giddy, that she even wanted to be that kind of woman. She hadn't expected to find her wedding moving, but she had. She couldn't see rushing to have another one.

Still, what she really kept thinking about was the limousine afterward, his hand beneath her skirt, his clever fingers moving through her wet heat—

Or maybe, came a voice inside her, *it's the sex part you don't know how to handle.*

She blew out a breath. And dived into a related topic she really had no interest whatsoever in discussing. The innocence she'd held on to all this time, without even meaning to. Not really. The innocence she was suddenly horrified to imagine was the reason he had always looked at her with such disdain—since it was the very opposite of the sort of sophistication he was known for, wasn't it?

"Is the reason you didn't touch me again after what happened in the back of the car because…" Annika could feel embarrassment coil, hard and hot, deep inside her. "Is it because you could tell?"

He took his time turning his head so he could gaze upon her and she remembered, in a distant way, that she'd used to think that he looked brutal. That was how masculine he was. That was how intense he looked, always.

But these days all she saw was the stark beauty of the man. As if one taste of him had made it impossible for her to see anything else.

As if she'd imprinted on him.

Even when he raised those dark brows of his as if he couldn't believe what he was hearing. An expression he wore often in her presence, but it was amazing how differently she felt about it now. When she could still feel the press of his mouth to hers. When she could still feel his hard fingers, deep inside her.

"Let me hasten to assure you, Annika, that I have been perfectly able to discern a woman's pleasure for some time." His voice was icy, but his golden gaze was hot. "In my opinion, a man cannot call himself a man unless he is capable of making a woman happy. It is my understanding that American men…" Ranieri shrugged. "Perhaps they do not deserve to use the term."

That lined up with a great many things she'd heard over the years, particularly from her college friends.

But, "That isn't what I meant," she said. "Although it is interesting."

Fascinating, more like it. She was still slippery at the very thought of the pleasure he'd given her, and there was a part of her that simply wanted to beg him to do it again. To keep doing it. To make her feel things she'd had no idea could be like that. His hand wasn't like hers. It was so big. His fingers blunt and long.

He'd put them *inside* her.

She had to fight back a shudder, though she could feel goose bumps all over her anyway.

"What did you mean, then?" he asked, in that way he had that made her think he knew the location of each and every goose bump on her body. "What do you think I could tell besides the fact you came apart in my hands? And so beautifully?"

Annika would have to add that to the list of things she'd had no idea people could just…talk about. She'd read a lot of books, certainly, but it hadn't occurred to her that in real life, a man might actually say such things to a woman. Just sit here and *say* them.

And she realized she'd been too busy thinking it all through when those relentless gold eyes of his seemed to soften and he reached over to run his knuckles over her cheek.

That was also when she realized that she was blushing. A lot.

But she needed to take this seriously regardless of whether or not she was bright red, because she felt she had to make this declaration. She'd talked it over with her friends. There had been votes for and against. Some thought, given the realities of their relationship, that she wasn't required to tell him anything. She could simply… see how it all went. Others were convinced that Annika, personally, would like it better if there were no surprises. Though she wasn't sure she believed anything they said, because all of her friends seemed to think that Ranieri, renowned the world over for his many love affairs, would not react well to the news anyway.

I'm not sure that man has ever met another virgin in his life, one of her friends had said.

But then, Annika rather thought her friends wanted him to react badly and keep his distance as a result. They had all been united on one thing:

that the man who had been such a thorn in her side these last few years didn't deserve her.

Annika felt compelled to tell him anyway. Even if her friends were right that he would hate it.

Even if that means he never touches you again? a voice inside her asked.

It would be easy enough. Now was the time, before things…progressed. All she had to do was say it. *I'm a virgin.* Easy and to the point.

And she couldn't quite bring herself to open her mouth and do it.

"We are about to land," he told her, and for some reason, he sounded deeply amused. Possibly because he was the one who could *see* how she was blushing. "And we will have a bit of a drive. If you require more time to tell me whatever it is you wish to tell me, you have it." He ran that knuckle down her cheek again, then over her lips. "I cannot promise that I will be in a talking mood once we reach our destination. What I can promise you is that you will enjoy it, whatever happens."

"I don't have a lot of experience," she told him in a rush.

And then felt as if she might break into a sweat. Or possibly start crying. Maybe she already had.

He considered her for long moments, with that steady intensity that made everything within her seem to constrict. "And it was perhaps not so great, the little experience you have had."

She regarded him solemnly. "That is…not incorrect."

Ranieri looked down, then took her hand in his. "Annika. Hear me on this. I want you."

And that, too, astounded her. That he could simply…*say* such a thing. So baldly. And with such certainty.

More, he sounded as if it was normal. Run-of-the-mill. As if maybe a discussion of his needs was simply par for the course with him. She admired it. Maybe she was even the smallest bit jealous of it.

Annika felt her heart kick at her. So hard she was surprised it wasn't catapulting straight from her chest.

"This is not what we might have chosen, you and I," he said, in that low, stirring way he had. "But here we are. I already know that you want me, too. Handily, we are married to each other, like it or not. It seems to me that there are a great many ways that we might spend this year together. One of them is to enjoy each other as much as possible. What do you think?"

It was a variation of what he'd said to her before, but everything was so different now. She'd had much the same thought herself, hadn't she? More, she had walked down an aisle and made vows to him, in front of people she cared about. He had put his mouth against her neck and let his fingers find their way inside her. He had made her sob and writhe in his arms.

He had touched her face gently and looked at her as if even then, given his way, he would have preferred to devour her.

And now she found herself thinking too many things at once—

But mostly, she really, truly wanted to know what *enjoying him* might entail.

She wanted to know that with such intensity that it made her shake.

"I would like that," Annika told him quietly.

Because she loved her museum, but she wasn't an exhibit in it. She was alive. She would never have chosen any of this, but it was happening. It had already happened. He was her husband and she wanted to experience that in every possible way she could, for as long as she could. No matter what came next. And no matter how much she'd loathed him all these years.

The look he gave her then reminded her of the same expression he'd worn as he'd said his own vows. That intensity. That gravity.

As if all of that ruthlessness he wore so easily he would bring to bear here, too.

Something in her shook and shook at that notion.

Because even now, even though he'd had his hand between her legs and he'd spoken of things like *coming apart beautifully*, she still couldn't imagine—no matter how she tried—what it would truly be like to lie naked with this man, to feel him all over her, to welcome him deep inside her body. Only not his fingers this time.

Ranieri's eyes lit with a deep heat, and he laughed. And Annika knew then that he could read her every thought, all over her face.

"Steady on, *amore*," he murmured. "We have a little way to go yet."

But for Annika, everything shifted into a kind of overbright, sweet syrup of need and longing. And threaded through it all was a humming sort of anticipation. It seemed to take her over. She could feel it in her bones.

They landed in an airfield high in the hills. Outside, the air was crisp and the sky was a deep, moody blue, the last gasp of a fall night. Ranieri was the one who swung into the driver's seat of one of the vehicles that waited there. It was a smaller sort of SUV, the kind they liked in Europe, and Annika was not surprised to find that he drove it the way he did everything else. With that singular focus. That intense competence.

She thought she'd be perfectly happy to sit beside him forever and let him drive her wherever he wished them to go.

Because all she could think about was that growing hunger inside her. The fire was indistinguishable now from that ache, making her feel trembly. Everywhere.

And the terrible wanting that left her too close to breathless, like that was all that was left of her.

"I am not close to my family," he told her, unbidden, as the new day began to stir outside. She knew they were somewhere north of Milan as he drove her into the hills without consulting a map, moving swiftly along winding mountain roads he seemed to know the way he knew everything. As if the whole of the world was etched there on the back of his hand.

Even the valleys she glimpsed seemed a part of his singular magic—vineyards stretching toward the rising sun, medieval castles standing guard.

She was beginning to think she was a part of it, too.

"You don't have to talk about it," she said quietly. "Families can be complicated."

"Perhaps that is so. But I have always felt that mine was more complicated than most—or perhaps less inclined to pretend otherwise. My parents divorced long ago. And both of them are entirely too proud to admit that they might have borne any fault in the split. Then again, as their only child, I have long been entirely too proud myself and more, unwilling to admit that anything they did with their personal lives bothered me in the slightest."

She glanced over at him, then returned her gaze to the hills all around them, gleaming gold in the morning light. "You do know what they say about pride."

"I do indeed. And it has precipitated many a fall in my family, I assure you. I tell you this because we have come here and it is entirely possible that my parents will take it upon themselves to turn up. And if they do so together, well." He shrugged in that supremely Italian way of his that was mesmerizing enough in New York. Here, it seemed a part of the very landscape. "Anything might happen."

The roads grew more twisting and steep. Annika held fast to the door handle beside her and let what he'd said sink in.

"I don't suppose that your interest in proper behavior has anything to do with your parents, does it?" she asked quietly. "It doesn't sound as if you find them appropriate, either."

Ranieri let out a bark of laughter that seemed to surprise him as much as it did her. He took a sharp turn, the SUV seeming to hug the narrow road. "My grandmother was all that was graceful and refined.

My mother and father, not so much. I think you already know where I fall."

And he sounded the way he always did. Assured. Arrogant. Ranieri, through and through. And yet…

Annika didn't know how she dared, but she reached across and put her hand on his leg. Then felt the heat of him, of all that rock-hard strength. It seemed to flood her palm, making her want to do something more, like lean down and explore him. Possibly with her mouth, though surely that would kill them both on a road like this—

Focus, she ordered herself.

"Don't worry," she told him, sounding throatier than was wise, surely. "I would happily embarrass you in front of the entirety of New York City. But I would never do such a thing in front of your parents."

The sun was up now, so she could see with perfect clarity the faintly arrested expression on his face. He glanced over at her briefly, then dropped his gaze to where her hand rested on his leg.

She felt very nearly scalded as she went to pull her hand away.

But he stopped her easily enough by placing his hand over hers, trapping her there.

Annika told herself at once that she wasn't to torture herself with questions about what this might mean. She told herself to simply enjoy the heat of his thigh below her palm and the hard press of his palm against the back of her hand, too.

And she could not have said how long it was that they drove like that. She was lost in the motion of the car, the Italian countryside all around. The fact she was *touching* him. Eventually, he took a road that wound down into a charming valley. There was a river that cut through it, a lake at the center. And everywhere else there were fields turned golden, vineyards winding down into autumn, sturdy cypress trees like sentinels, and there, nestled in the middle of carpets of wildflowers, an old house.

It was built of ancient stone with a red roof and charming shutters. And it was not the sort of castle or fortress they'd seen along the way. It was prettier, as if someone had taken the old stones and determinedly made them over into a home. Yet it still had the feel of something suitably medieval as they drove closer, and Ranieri finally pulled to a stop in the pebbled courtyard in front.

"This is my grandmother's cottage," he told her, his voice gone rough. He turned to her, still holding her hand beneath his. "She left it to me when she passed."

"It's beautiful," Annika whispered.

It was more than beautiful. It looked like a fairy tale. It made her wish she believed that fairy tales could be real. It made her wish—

But no. She stopped herself there. It wasn't safe to lose herself in all these *wishes* when there was only a year. Only one, solitary year.

"I have come here many times," Ranieri told her in that same gruff way, as if he didn't know how to say these things. As if they were torn from within him. "I cannot always be in cities, you understand. But what I need you to know, Annika, is that I have never brought another woman here. Ever. You're the first." Something seemed to swell between them, then. "The only."

And she could feel that fluttery beat inside her. Her pulse. Her heart. Her relentless longing. All of her, lost somewhere between a shudder and a sob, no matter how dangerous it was.

She understood, very distinctly, that this was an offering. His wedding gift, perhaps. That he could not give her innocence. He could not erase her father's demands that had brought them here. He could not give her anything other than what he was—all that he was.

But he could bring her here.

To this far-off valley that meant something to him. To this old, beloved house, nestled in fields of flowers and flanked by ancient columns of cypress. She could see that this made him vulnerable, though she knew better than to use that word. For men like him, it could only be taken as an insult. Even now, when he had done this deliberately.

Still, she knew. She could feel it in the heat of his hand, the hard stone of his thigh. She could see it in his gaze, gold and intense.

And she knew with a deep, feminine certainty that she would walk through the doors of this enchanted place, give herself to this man, and be forever changed.

In this moment, gazing into his rich, golden eyes as a beautiful Italian morning danced all around them, that felt like a bargain.

"Ranieri," she whispered. "I want you."

And when he laughed, it was a dark, thrilling sound.

If there was vulnerability in him then, she did not see it any longer. He slammed out of the car and rounded the front of it, opening her door and pulling her out with so much obvious, leashed strength that it only made her aware of how in control of himself he'd been all this time.

How in control he always was.

Her feet hardly touched the ground before he swept her into his arms again, and then he was striding forward, shouldering his way into the house and carrying her over the threshold.

She clung to him, having no idea how she could focus on the details of the house as he moved through it so swiftly. He carried her up a set of stairs and down another corridor, but all she could really see was the stark sensuality in his expression. A certain kind of grimness that translated directly into a bright heat inside her, spiraling all around until she ached even more, there between her legs.

And then, suddenly, she was in the air. Then bouncing on a mattress, and she couldn't help but laugh.

Ranieri followed her down, and then there was no more room for laughter. Everything crystallized into that blistering heat.

Finally, she thought. Maybe she said it.

Her clothes came off easily, soft cashmere and smooth wool no match for his touch, for the cleverness of his fingers. His mouth was on hers, then on her neck, and then he followed the curves of her body, pausing as he liked to taste her, to tempt her.

But before he could settle into any one of the places that longed for him, Annika was pushing against him. She made him sit up and then, however inexpertly, she set about pulling his clothes from his body until he laughed, pushed her away, and handled it himself.

Annika knelt there, gaping as he was finally revealed to her.

On some level, she had expected the perfection of his chest. The dark hair dusted over the impossible glory of his chest, his ridged abdomen. She'd expected that, yes—but she hadn't really understood *how* perfect he was.

Or how the act of looking at him could make her whole body quiver with excitement.

Especially when her gaze was drawn to that male part of him, heavy and low between his legs. It made her feel something like drunk. And when she lifted her gaze to his again, he wore a grin that reminded her of nothing so much as a wolf.

"I intended to finesse this," he told her in a low voice. "We will have time for that. Later."

"I want you," Annika said again, because she understood, now, the power in those words. The beauty in them. Their stark, simple truth.

Ranieri made a low, deep sound that seemed ripped from inside him. And then he was crawling over her, kissing her everywhere, his hands touching, taunting, tearing her into pieces, each touch making her want him more than the last.

She wrapped herself around him, and experimented with pressing her greedy breasts against his chest, rubbing them a little this way, then that, to feel his hard, hair-roughened muscles against them.

And she shuddered so hard at the sensation that she almost thought—

"Wait for me," he ordered her, there against her mouth.

Annika was dimly aware of it when he reached for protection, and rolled it on, but everything was a clamoring riot within her now. Everything was so sharp, so hungry.

He reached down, guiding himself through her heat, a hard grin glimmering on his face when he made her moan. When he made her buck up against him, and try to force him to...*do something*. Because she knew there was something. Something more—

But then he thrust deep inside her, and everything shattered—

And she knew.

She finally knew.

Ranieri gathered her against him and held her there as he worked himself deep inside her, again and again.

And she couldn't tell what *finesse* could have added to this, because it was everything he was— and more.

It was so raw. It was so *male*. It was a glorious ferocity and she felt its glorious teeth inside her. It was a cresting wave that never quite broke, or always broke, and made her want to do animal things, like dig her nails into his skin. Bite his shoulder.

And when she did those things, following some deep, inner feminine savagery, he made deep noises of approval, and thrust harder. Deeper.

Annika sobbed out his name, a terrible, wonderful wave rolling over her. She arched up against him, and he laughed.

Then did it again.

And again.

Until everything inside her became a storm and when she flew apart, she heard him call out her name.

Then follow her, straight into all that sweet fury, as if it was who they'd been all along.

As if he'd known who they were from the start.

Annika took a long while to come back into her own body, there in a bed in a strange room, far away from New York and the life that she'd known.

And no longer the innocent she'd been.

No longer innocent at all... And she had expected such a momentous thing to feel complicated. She had heard so many terrible stories. Even some supposedly good stories that had lingered over the mechanical issues of the act. She had expected tears, and a great deal of *I'm a woman now*, but all she felt was...*wonderful*.

She could barely rouse herself. She wasn't sure she ever wanted to move again. And then when she did, she found Ranieri gazing back at her. Gold eyes and dark hair, and a possessive look on his sensual face.

And as she watched, a slow, hot sort of smile spread across his mouth.

"I think we can say we have well and truly taken the edge off," he said, his voice a low rasp.

Then he was crawling over her, pulling her with him. And to her utter shock, Annika felt those same wildfires burn bright in her anew.

"Now," Ranieri said in his sternest voice, kissing his way down the length of her body and settling himself between her legs, only looking up to flash a bit of that gold at her before returning his attention to the part of her that wanted him most, "why don't we do this properly."

CHAPTER EIGHT

NOTHING COULD HAVE PREPARED Annika for her honeymoon.

The days were warm, golden bright, and perfect. The nights were cool and called for fires in the grate and long walks in the vineyards, her head tipped back to take in the sky sloppy with stars. He had brought his trusted staff with him from New York and they managed to be both efficient and mostly invisible. It was at mealtimes that she was most grateful that they were here, heaping the bounty of this enchanted valley before them, so that there was no part of her day or night that was not a feast.

If this was the marriage her father had wanted for her, she was only astonished that he hadn't hurried her into it sooner. Had he known all along? She hoped so.

Because this was magic.

Ranieri was magic.

Annika couldn't get enough of him. No matter how many times he took her in the night, she woke up starving for more. No matter how he spread her before him, letting the golden light dance all over her naked body, she wanted to give him more.

There was nothing she wouldn't give him, she thought after a week had passed, a soft, hot rush of sensation and delight. She only grew more voracious. She only wanted more. There was no sensual banquet she wasn't prepared to share with him.

Their days took on an easy routine. They tended to wake at the first hint of light, turning to each other in that wide bed they'd claimed as theirs. It sat at the back of the house, so that sometimes Annika imagined that she could hear her own cries echo back to her from the hills beyond. And no matter how wild or adventurous they'd gotten the night before, their mornings were always about fire. Need.

As if, she sometimes thought, neither one of them could believe that this was real.

Ranieri usually left her to spend his morning in the cottage's study, tending to his empire from afar. But Italian mornings were early in New York, so Annika allowed herself to be lazy. Sometimes she got up when Ranieri did, but more often she turned over and dozed.

She would have been the first to say that she'd led too privileged a life to have earned her idle-

ness, and some mornings, the guilt of that had her
charging out of bed. But as the days passed, she felt
less and less guilty. She couldn't remember losing
her mother, yet the loss had marked her whole life.
Losing her father had been two terrible days, with
five years of a slower, more pervasive grief in between. The day of his accident and the day of his
death had been unbearable in their own ways, especially because she'd had all that time in the middle
to let herself imagine that things might be different. So much time that his death had been a shock,
when perhaps she should have seen it as a blessing.

Because he was free now.

It was only here, across the ocean in Italy, on a
honeymoon with the least likely man alive, that Annika found the space to let herself mourn.

Maybe it was because she wasn't fighting it here.
Maybe it was because she simply let whatever emotions came up wash over her in this place of golden
ease. It was grief, but it was sweeter, somehow, than
it might have been otherwise.

When she finally rose in the mornings, she took
her time in the bath, or in the shower. Often, she
would find herself staring out the windows until
the beauty of the small, perfect valley overwhelmed
her and she would feel drawn to take long walks
through the fields.

And as she walked, she thought about…everything. Her lost mother she hoped she resembled in as many ways as possible. Her father, who had loved her so. His confounding will, which seemed to refute that. The past month and a half. And Ranieri, who was so tangled up in all of it.

Some days he would come and find her out in the fields when it was getting toward midday. He would grin at her, that dark, fierce face of his set in such bold lines. He would tumble her down into the sweet grass or the soft earth, and teach her new ways to cry out. To hold that beauty in her hands and chase the wildness that was only theirs.

Other times she wandered back to the house, and would take a light lunch with him on the patio outside his study, if the weather was fine. Or inside near the fire if it was cool. And they would talk. The way they never had in all the years they'd known each other, stretching back to when she'd been a teenager. Not necessarily of big, emotional things, but all the rest of it. Small stories. Observations. The connective tissue that held all the big things together, she liked to think.

Like they were just people. Not enemies making the best of things.

Over lunch one day, she made some comment about needing to find more ways to teach him a lesson or two. Ranieri gazed at her with laughter all over his face and his eyes bright. And no matter how many times she saw it these days, it never failed to make her breath catch.

"I'm happy to teach you jujitsu," he said after a moment. "Though I cannot promise that I will teach you to be any good at it."

"I've actually taken a jujitsu class before." Annika wrinkled up her nose. "It seemed like a whole lot of very dramatic cuddling."

He stared across the brightly tiled table at her, looking as outraged as he did astonished. *"Cuddling,"* he repeated.

"All that clenching together. And then writhing about everywhere. You know, it all seemed like a lot of *thighs*." She shook her head. "And then quite a bit of heaving about. It was off-putting, I have to say."

Ranieri continued to stare at her for a moment. Then he reached over, plucking her out of her chair and pulling her over his lap.

"Perhaps you need another lesson," he murmured, nipping at her chin and making her shiver.

But what he taught her then, carrying her into the study and laying her down on the thick rug like an offering, was not jujitsu. Or any martial art Annika had ever heard of.

It was glorious all the same.

In the afternoons, she liked to check in with the museum back at home. Then she usually found a book and curled up with it, loving the afternoons when Ranieri ignored his own work, sought her out, and took her back to bed. But loving just as much the peaceful hours she got to spend in her favorite chair, sometimes dozing, sometimes unable to turn the pages fast enough.

And always, at some point, thinking back to when he'd brought up sex and she'd wondered what *regular sex* might even look like.

They dressed for dinner every night, and the dressing itself sometimes took longer than necessary. Because Ranieri's "help" always ended the same way—with him surging deep inside her as they both took their pleasure, because the real magic was the way they fit together.

That friction. That heat.

His hardness so deep in her softness, his mouth ravaging her neck, her breasts. Her nails leaving marks on his shoulders, his back.

It only seemed to get worse, this need. This endless wanting.

Sometimes they had their dinner outside, taking advantage of the last of the mild nights. When it was colder—and it kept getting colder—they sat in the cottage's pleasant dining room, or took trays before the fire of their choice. And always there was the sensual delight of the food they ate. Every night it was a feast of local fare, prepared to perfection. But for Annika, the real treat was the opportunity to get to know this man who had cast his shadow over her life for so long.

She knew better than to say out loud some of the conclusions she'd come to during her lazy mornings or out on her long walks. She knew better than to say that clearly, her father had known what he was doing here. That he'd been on to something. That he'd seen something in them that neither one of them would ever have come to on their own.

After all, Ranieri had only signed up for a year. Annika might already be hoping that they would last longer than that, but she wasn't foolish enough to say that. She didn't want to ruin the year he was willing to give her.

Because she wanted every greedy, glorious moment of it.

"Tell me about your grandmother," she said one night, when one week had turned into two, and kept rolling on. "She's the one you speak of most often."

Tonight they were seated not in the cottage's formal dining room, but one of the smaller sitting rooms. Like everything else in this lovely house, it was furnished in light, pleasing shades. The fire in the grate seemed to dance lovingly over the carefully placed objects that graced the tables, the precisely arranged stacks of books, and the quietly impressive art that was hung haphazardly over each wall.

Like every other room in this house, the elegance of the surroundings never took away from the room's comfort. Even if the previous owner hadn't been Ranieri's grandmother, Annika would have been curious how anyone had managed to pull that off. She assured herself it was a professional interest, given she was the one responsible for staging the exhibits at the museum.

Ranieri sat back in his chair, the last of the night's meal before them. They had eaten at a small round table that allowed them to sit closer to each other and he had fed her morsels throughout from his fingers, adding a glimmering undercurrent of fire to every bite she took.

And now that fire was banked, though still in his gaze as he held his wineglass and swirled it in his hand, taking a moment to glance around the room.

"Everyone told my grandmother that she was making a bad bet on one of those Furlans," he said after a moment or two passed. "That it would all end in tears. But she defied them and did it anyway, to her sorrow."

"Are you all so bad, then?" Annika smiled when his gaze moved back to hers, even though he looked remote again. "I thought it was only you."

She was used to him smiling more these days. There was that crook in the corner of his mouth, but it went beyond that, too. Sometimes he grinned widely, the autumn sun pouring all over him as if the grin had summoned it. He laughed more and more as the days went by, usually a wicked, sensual sound, there against her skin.

The world might have been spinning them into another winter's darkness, but between them, the light only grew.

Yet she was reminded that he was still Ranieri Furlan as he gazed back across the table now, his expression taking on that grave, grim coldness she knew so well. Even if she hadn't seen it since they'd left New York.

And maybe it told her everything she needed to know about herself that seeing it now only made her shiver with delight. It made her want him, as if she had never had him at all.

It made her wonder why, exactly, she had told herself she hated him all these years. All these long years when he had always looked at her this way. When he had always been so inaccessible, so remote.

And all the while, there'd been this hunger deep inside her, just waiting for him to feed it.

But she had asked him a question and he was answering it. She tried to squirm in her chair unobtrusively.

"It is not that we are bad in the ways you might imagine," he told her, his gaze dark. "On the contrary, we usually do quite well for ourselves. But sooner or later, we are presented with choices. And almost without exception, we choose our own pride over everything else."

"You have to give me examples, Ranieri." He had mentioned *pride* before, she was certain. But... "Pride can mean anything."

She thought she saw his jaw tense. Or maybe she only wanted the excuse to reach over and touch him, to soothe him... But she kept herself from it, curling her fingers around the delicate stem of her own wineglass instead. Though she hardly needed intoxicants when she was in his presence.

"Take my grandfather," Ranieri said, sounding distressingly cold and sober. "My grandmother was descended from Florentine nobility. She could have chosen anyone, yet she had eyes only for him. And this was a different time, you understand. So no matter their affection for each other, it was accepted practice that a man of my grandfather's station would secure the family line, then seek his pleasures where he chose."

"Mistresses," Annika said, though the word tasted bitter on her tongue. "You can just say the word."

Ranieri's eyes gleamed in a way that sent a cold shiver down the length of her spine. "My grandfather had only one mistress then. By all accounts, she was magnificent. The toast of Italy. There was not a man alive who did not want her."

Ranieri returned his attention to the room. More specifically, to the mantel above the fireplace. She followed his darkening gaze to a set of framed photographs and took the moment to study them. The dark-haired woman, laughing in one photo but too serious in the next.

Annika could see Ranieri in her face.

She felt a strange little tickle then, a kind of foreboding, and wanted almost desperately to stop this conversation. She knew how she would do it. She could launch herself across the table, then sink to her knees and take him in her mouth the way he'd taught her.

It would be a distraction, perhaps. But it would also make them both happy. She knew that as well as she knew her own name.

But she didn't dare do it. She didn't quite dare.

He was opening up to her, and no matter how being naked with him moved her, no matter what it showed her about the both of them, Annika understood that this was real vulnerability. That him telling her stories could never be dismissed as *just sex*.

A stray memory moved in her then, of her reaction when he'd told her that he had not initially intended to be faithful in this marriage. How outraged she'd been at the very idea, and that had been long before she'd developed this unhealthy, possessive fixation on his body.

On *him*.

She did not want to be married to any man who kept a mistress. And she specifically did not want to share Ranieri with anyone.

But she did not need to risk saying those things out loud, because she already knew she had no right to feel them. That was not what this was. That was not what they'd agreed. This one, miraculous year.

She cleared her throat. "I take it your grandmother was not pleased with this arrangement," she said instead.

"My grandmother was raised to accept these things as all women of her class did," Ranieri said, his voice seeming to grow darker and more forbidding by the word. "At first, it did not occur to her to object to what was common practice. But then she made the critical error of falling in love."

"With your grandfather?" Annika asked, hesitantly.

"He was in love with her, too," Ranieri said, but he sounded almost bitter. "She bore him a son, then two more. Both of them always said that those were happy years. Who knows how long that could have continued? But instead, my grandmother asked my grandfather to give up this mistress of his."

"That doesn't seem unreasonable."

Ranieri let out a laugh, too dark to be anything like amusement, and she knew the difference now. "Perhaps not. But then, my grandfather was a Furlan. There was no question that he loved my grandmother. He said so at the time. He loved his sons as well. But he would not be told by his wife that he should give up anything. He would not permit my grandmother to dictate his behavior. So they lived apart until they died, as he would not divorce her. And he not only kept his mistress, he took others to prove he could. He wasted a fortune on each, leaving my grandmother to fend for herself. Leaving her to raise his sons with the money she had brought into the marriage. He felt he could do as he liked, and so he did. What is that if not egregious pride? And how many lives marred because of it?"

Annika's heart was kicking at her, as if this was perilous, this conversation. She could not see how, seeing as they were speaking of people long dead. But she could feel the danger. She felt as if she was standing on the edge of a steep cliff and the wind was high.

"Still, my grandfather is not the best example of the Furlan pride," Ranieri continued. "His sins were only ever of a personal nature. There are far too many others who made certain that their stumbles ruined more than their marriages and families."

"With all these cautionary tales, you must have

spent your life doing your best to rid yourself of this pride," Annika said.

Perhaps too hopefully.

His dark brows rose. "Quite the opposite. I am so proud, Annika, that I refuse to accept that I will lose anything I wish to keep. My father has lost at least three fortunes by my reckoning. One of my uncles lost his life, too proud to admit he made a mistake and too proud to recognize that he was on the wrong side of the wrong kind of people. My other uncle considers himself too good to do what he ought to do to better his situation, an abominable display of misplaced pride if ever there was one. But as for me?" He did something with his glass of wine that seemed to take in the whole of the room, the cottage, perhaps the world. Certainly her. "I have made so many fortunes that it cannot matter if I lose three. Or even ten. Call it insurance if you will."

But he did not sound pleased by this. He sounded wrecked, and she hated it.

"Ranieri," she whispered. "Surely you must know—"

"I will show you what I know best," he told her then, his voice dark and grave.

But when he moved, coming to pull her out of her chair, his kiss lit them both on fire.

And he made love to her like a man possessed that night. First there on the couch in that sitting room. Then he carried her upstairs, spent some time with her in the spacious bath, and then ripped her to shreds in their bed.

Again and again.

Annika thrilled to it all.

He was ruthless and demanding, and she felt as if she'd been made for this. Made for him, to meet his need, his hunger. To match his ruthlessness with her own.

To make certain that both of them burned bright and long, together.

And in the morning, she woke as he surged inside her once more, framing her face with his big, restless hands, his gaze pinning her to the mattress in the early morning light.

Usually their mornings were flash fires, bold and bright and fast-moving, but today was different.

He moved slow, setting them both to smoldering. So slow that every thrust took forever, and every retreat felt like a loss.

Still, he held her gaze. Still, he held her face in his hands.

With every deep, beautiful thrust, he broke her heart.

And when it was done, Annika lay in the bed and understood that she was already repeating the mistake his grandmother had made.

She was in love with him. Irrevocably, unpardonably, and not at all *temporarily* in love.

And looking back, she thought as she sat in the bath again—sinking down until her whole body was submerged by the warm water, save her face—it was possible she always had been.

More than possible. Likely.

This morning's lovemaking had stripped away the last of her defenses, and she could see everything so clearly now. She had met him when she was barely sixteen and had hated the very sight of him—but what use could she possibly have had for silly boys after a sight of Ranieri? She'd gone on to college, where so many of her friends had experimented with passion and longing, crushes and relationships, but never Annika.

Some part of her must have known all along that she could settle for no substitutes. Even though she'd continued to despise him. Even though she'd considered him the bane of her existence.

Maybe there had been something in her that had sensed the kind of fire they would kindle together, all along.

"It's all right," she assured herself as she rose from the bath and got dressed in her walking clothes, an easy pair of soft overalls, a chambray shirt, a wide-brimmed hat. "It's all going to be all right."

Because it was clear to her that last night's storytelling had indeed been a cautionary tale—but for her, not him.

She stopped by the portrait of his grandmother that hung in the hall outside their bedroom. "I will not make the same mistake you did," she promised this woman long gone, who had been punished for her heart. "I won't tell him."

Though she understood why the other woman had made the choice she had. Annika could feel her heart beating too fast. She could *feel* her own heart. And she knew that there was nothing more she wanted to tell Ranieri than the truth.

Even though she knew he wouldn't take it well.

She would hold it inside. She would keep it sacred, and hers. And as long as she didn't say it, she didn't see why she couldn't have this year of theirs.

And maybe more than this year, a voice in her whispered, because in everything concerning this man, she was so greedy. So interminably greedy. *If you play your cards right.*

Annika almost laughed at that as she made her way down the stairs, heading toward Ranieri's study on autopilot. Because when had she ever been even remotely good at cards?

Well, she would have to learn. And in the meantime, she would take all these new, unwieldy feelings and keep them where they belonged. Deep inside her. Hidden away, like treasures too precious to be taken out in the light.

She could do it, she was sure.

Or in any event, she *would* do it.

But when she pushed open the door to Ranieri's study, she didn't have to worry that he might see her love for him all over her face.

Because he wasn't alone.

And she was certain she knew exactly who the two older people were who sat there on the couch of the study, neither one of them looking pleased. If she looked closely, she was certain she could see the man she loved in both of them.

Her gaze flew to Ranieri as he stood there at the mantel, looking...cold and cruel.

As distant as if none of these sweet honeymoon days had ever happened.

"*Buongiorno*, Annika," he said, but not in the way he normally said her name. Not with that dark delight she'd come to depend on. "How kind of you to join us. May I present my parents. It appears they have invited themselves along on our honeymoon."

CHAPTER NINE

RANIERI TOLD HIMSELF he was grateful.

Grateful that he had not spoken this morning, so deep inside Annika's body that he had somehow felt that he was turned inside out. He had not said the things he knew he shouldn't. He had fought back all those strange and terrible feelings that had broken loose after their conversation the night before. When he had never wished to speak to her of *pride* at all.

That was not the word he wanted to use, not when he came to Annika. This woman who took everything he threw at her, wrapped it up in endless delight, and then asked for more.

In his whole life, Ranieri had never met anyone who did not grow weary of his intensity. He had never spent this amount of unrestricted time with a woman. Or with anyone. He had learned long ago that he was better—more effective, even—in small doses. He had come to think of that as a virtue.

But then there was Annika, who had all but lived in his skin for weeks now, and showed no signs at all of wanting or needing a break.

If anything, she seemed to want more.

She was a wonder.

And he had nearly opened his mouth and said the kinds of things he couldn't take back.

The kind of things that would ruin them.

So really, all things considered, he found himself profoundly grateful that his parents had arrived, unannounced, this morning of all mornings.

His mother, the perpetually dissatisfied Paola, did not openly sneer at her new, American daughter-in-law. Instead, she only treated Annika to a slow perusal, from head to toe and back again, making it clear that she was not impressed with what she saw. "I see that you've taken to country life with enthusiasm," she said.

Ranieri wanted to take his mother apart for that snide tone. But before he could find a way to do that without also showing how much he cared about Annika—information his mother would only use as ammunition, which he could not allow—Annika herself laughed.

"You must forgive me," she said, her voice warm and something like merry. "I'm on my way to my morning walk out in the fields. I had no idea Ranieri was entertaining or I would have changed into something more appropriate."

She glanced down at her clothes as if she'd been off rolling around in the dirt when she looked the way she always did. Beautiful. Natural and unstudied, and Ranieri thought that Paola, with her penciled-on brows and dark grooves of disappointment bracketing her lips, would do well to take a page from Annika's book.

"Your mother has apparently come here to make uncivil remarks," said his father. "I did not."

Giuseppe Furlan looked more like his only son than Ranieri cared to acknowledge. Because looking at his father was always like looking into a kind of fun house mirror. It was a view of the future, but a future that required that Ranieri make a certain set of unpalatable choices. To be embittered, always. To make the same mistakes again and again. And to blame others instead of himself, forever. If he took care to do those things then Ranieri was sure to find himself with those same stooped shoulders and his father's indignant chin.

A fate worse than death, Ranieri had long believed.

Giuseppe barely even glanced at Annika, its own insult. "I have a very important investment opportunity I need to speak to you about, Ranieri. This is a business call."

Ranieri offered what he hoped passed for some kind of a smile, though it felt far too harsh. "Perhaps you both missed the news," he said, a deep chill in his voice. "I am on my honeymoon. This is my wife. You appear to have forgotten to offer us your felicitations. An oversight, I am certain."

"I had no idea you were even getting married," his mother said querulously, but with enough heat that he suspected he'd hit upon her true reason for coming here today. "How do you think that made me look? You didn't even think to invite your own *mother*!"

There were a great many things Ranieri could have said to that, all of them unkind. But instead, Annika went and sat next to his mother on the couch, reminding him that despite the way high society New York liked to talk about Bennett Schuyler's supposedly shameful daughter, she was, in fact, the consummate hostess. Her manners were exquisite. Here, when it counted, not out there in public where everything most people did was a bid for status and points.

"It happened so quickly," Annika was saying. "And it's all my fault. My father died so suddenly, you see. He'd been in a coma for a long while, and then there at the end…well. I didn't see it coming." She kept smiling in that engaging way of hers, despite the sour expression Paola offered her in return.

"Our wedding was very quick and very small. But you must forgive Ranieri. I'm sure that he wanted to wait until his whole family was there, but it wasn't possible."

Ranieri stood there, battling warring urges within him. He wanted to throw his parents out. But then, he always did. He wanted to protect Annika, even though he knew if he did that, his parents would focus on her in a way he knew he *really* wouldn't like.

And beneath all of that, he wanted to live in the version of their story that Annika was telling. Where everything between them was clean and new and theirs. No wills, no games of one-upmanship. Only a man and a woman who had rushed to marry because they wanted each other that badly.

What did it say about him that he wanted that to be real?

It should have shaken him that here in this cottage, so far away from reality, he had almost convinced himself that it was.

"Congratulations on your union," Giuseppe said grudgingly. His cold eyes moved over Annika, then dismissed her. Another insult Ranieri would have dearly liked to address, but that was the trouble with his parents. Calling attention to their behavior only made it worse. "I'm certain the wedding was charming. How nice. But I would really like to talk to you about this investment. This one is a sure thing."

Ranieri stood there, frozen at the mantel. His parents were playing their usual games, here in this cottage that was all things elegant and graceful but was still nothing more than a monument his grandmother had built to her own loneliness.

And he felt nothing but dirty.

He might thunder on about the Furlan pride, but pride wasn't what he felt when he was around these people. It was this other thing.

They were a stain and he had never been able to wash it clean.

And he might have tried to conceal that stain with money, businesses, properties, too many women. He might have found ways to pretend.

But at the end of the day, it always came down to this. His mother's inability to think of anyone or anything but herself. His father's obvious feeling of entitlement to his son's hard-earned and long-kept wealth. When he'd been young, the details might have been different but the end result had always been the same. Anything he did was an insult to his mother, if she chose to take it that way, and whatever it was had to be scrutinized to see if it might be an opportunity for his father to leverage his own interests.

They had never cared about anything else. He

knew that despite their divorce the two of them met regularly to discuss all the ways Ranieri had let them down and what they could do to force him into line. This cottage was his favorite place on the planet, but he only used it sparingly, because they had their spies in this valley and they always descended upon him here.

He would have said he'd grown immune to them.

But today, in the middle of the same old story sat Annika. His Annika, looking fresh and pretty and entirely his.

And she did not belong here, with them, where they could get that stain on her, too. The certainty of that was like concrete, falling through him like so much stone.

Yet he understood it now, what had happened last night. What he'd almost said this morning. Annika made him feel clean. She made him imagine that there was something more to him than his father's grift and his mother's complaints. Of all the women he had ever been with, Annika was the one who should have wanted him least. And she was the one who'd asked him for nothing.

It was no wonder at all that she was the only one he wanted. The only one he could not be without.

For it was clear to him now, standing in this study while his parents began to bicker and Annika sat between them looking serene, that there was no reason he should have adhered to even one of the stipulations attached to that will. It might have been inconvenient to start over, but as he'd told Annika already, that was what he excelled at. That was what he did.

He didn't need the Schuyler Corporation at all.

But he was very much afraid he might need her.

And it was not lost on him that acknowledging this now, with his sordid past on excruciating display, was as good as not acknowledging it at all. And no matter that the admission made everything inside him seem to slide off the side of the planet, even if he made it only to himself.

"You always do this," his mother was saying shrilly to his father. "You always try to cut me out. I won't let you do it this time."

"I owe you nothing, woman," Giuseppe retorted, with a snort of laughter. "You've already sucked me dry."

He remembered Annika telling him what he was sure he already knew on some level, but could see with such unfortunate clarity now. That obviously this display was why he put such stock in good breeding, good manners, and the trappings of civility. Like proper dress, as if allowing so much as a tendril to break free from a chignon signaled the end of civilization.

Because, after all, that was what he knew. Anything could set either one of them off, and then they were here again. In this swamp of accusation and threat, insult and anger.

His childhood in a nutshell.

"Ranieri," his father all but bellowed. "You really must give me a few moments of your attention. Have you no head for business?"

"Ranieri," shrieked his mother, not to be outdone, "what kind of unnatural son are you, to hate your own mother so much that you would not only bar me from your wedding, but ignore me in your own home?"

And he felt something inside him, like a cracking. Maybe it was a shattering.

Whatever it was, it was as clarifying as it was unpleasant.

Across from him, it was as if Annika could read what was happening. As if she alone could read *him*, when he would have sworn no one could. She stood, smiling at Paola and Giuseppe in turn.

"How wonderful that you could come to catch up," she said smoothly, as if that was something either one of them would ever think to do. "I'll have a light lunch put together, so we can all enjoy each other's company." She nodded at Giuseppe. "Why don't you stay here and have a little chat with Ranieri. This is the perfect time." Then she smiled encouragingly at Paola. "I'm not ashamed to say this is a bit overwhelming for me. Maybe you can come and show me how it's done?"

His mother looked back and forth between them, as if deciding whether or not she was winding up to pitch a larger fit. But her sense of her own magnificence won out, as it usually did. Because she enjoyed nothing more than telling others how they were doing things wrong. He imagined she would enjoy it even more than usual, here in his house.

Ranieri wanted to pull Annika to him. He wanted to kiss her mouth again and lose himself there, because he had the sinking feeling that kisses like that were limited. More limited than he might have imagined before his parents had turned up here today.

Instead he had to settle for her smile as she led Paola away.

He had to watch her leave him, looking wholly at her ease, as if she could think of nothing better to do than spend time with a woman so toxic that Ranieri had never known her to have a single friend. Not one. If he had not seen the photographs of his mother when she was young and almost ethereally beautiful, he would have assumed that she'd somehow blackmailed his father into marriage.

The truth, he knew, was worse. They had been mad for each other, but all that heat had turned into hatred.

It was a lesson Ranieri had no desire to learn.

After the door closed behind the women, his father launched into his latest ridiculous pitch, but all Ranieri could think about was Annika.

Because he understood now that he had no choice. He needed to end this.

It had already gone too far.

Later that evening, he waited for her in the small sitting room off their bedroom, a bright sanctuary he remembered from his childhood. This cottage had been his refuge. Here, his grandmother was an interested yet soothing authority figure—a far cry from his parents. His grandmother had liked to sit here to catch the afternoon light on her needlework and he'd always joined her, when he was still small enough to lie before her on the floor, or pretend to read his own book at her side.

I wish I could live here forever, he had said, more than once.

But she had always responded the same way. *It is true that home is where you make it,* she'd replied. *But sometimes we are drawn to places because they permit us to hide.* And she had looked at him, her brown eyes so wise. *But we are Furlans, you and I, for good or ill. Much as we might wish to hide forever, we know we can't.*

Ranieri had remembered those words his whole life. He had used them as a guide.

He hid from nothing. He faced everything head-on, always.

Or he had, until Annika.

So there was no one he could blame this on but him.

Perhaps that made him colder when Annika finally came upstairs after the interminable dinner with his mother was finally done, and Paola had been packed off to a car that he hoped would take her far, far away from here.

His father had left in a rage much earlier, after Ranieri's typical, inevitable refusal to invest in anything he brought to the table. The good news about that was that it had left one fewer parent to remind Ranieri of his own shortcomings. The bad news was that the remaining parent was Paola.

And even though he could have recited her many litanies of victimization by heart, every word she'd uttered had seemed like a nail in the coffin of Ranieri's marriage. One after the next, all evening long. Because his mother managed to pollute a place as impossibly graceful as his grandmother's house with her usual poison. He didn't think she had even been trying all that hard. It was that easy for her.

What made him think that he wouldn't do the same thing, given time?

How could he imagine that he could hold on to something as clean and bright as Annika? He knew what would happen if he did. He would be the one to get his grubby fingerprints all over her. He would be the one to turn her around, taking all that bright defiance and greedy need and turning it sour.

He did not think he could bear it.

"You're never in here," came her happy voice from behind him, and when he turned, she was smiling at him.

So artlessly. So easily. The wedding at her museum had changed everything. Before that, he knew she'd been desperate to embarrass him enough that he'd break it off. After that, she'd been his.

Maybe that museum of hers was enchanted after all.

But the trouble was, Ranieri did not believe in enchantments. He believed in evidence. And he had a preponderance of that, all of it pointing in the same direction.

That still didn't mean he wanted to do this.

"Why are you looking at me like that?" Annika asked, her voice soft even as a frown gathered between her eyes.

He waited. She blinked, then looked around the sitting room. And he knew the precise moment she saw her own bags, packed and waiting. She sucked in a breath.

"Are we going on a trip?" she asked.

Ranieri was known for never hesitating. For always shooting to kill, never waiting to see what might happen first. But he knew that there would always be a *before* and *after* this moment. And he wasn't ready to be done with the before.

If he'd known that this morning would be the end this thing between them, he wouldn't have changed a thing. But perhaps he would have savored it even more.

"I'm going to Shanghai," he told her, sounding too dark. Too stiff. "You're going to New York."

Her frowned deepened. She threaded her fingers together before her and he knew, by now, how that little gesture betrayed her unease. A month ago, he wouldn't have cared. Tonight, it moved in him like anguish. But it changed nothing.

"I always knew this couldn't last forever, Ranieri." Her voice was calm. Smooth. It was precisely why he had to do this now, before she couldn't maintain her composure in his presence. Before they were no better than Giuseppe and Paola, so committed to their own misery they didn't care who witnessed it. "But why are you announcing the end of our honeymoon like this?"

"It has been nearly three weeks. I think we both know that there was only so long I can continue to ignore my responsibilities."

That furrow between her brows deepened. "I have responsibilities, too. Not that it's a competition. But the point of a honeymoon is to take a break from them."

"You leave within the hour," he told her shortly. "I will have a driver take you to the airfield. You'll be back in New York before you know it."

Her green eyes narrowed slightly. "You say that as if more than our honeymoon is ending."

And he'd known she wouldn't be satisfied. He'd known she would ask. There was no possibility that she was ever going to get on that plane without demanding to know his feelings—even if she would never ask about his feelings directly.

Ranieri had come to know this woman entirely too well. That was part of the problem.

"We've already stayed here too long," he said, in forbidding tones. "My parents have little to recommend them, but neither one of them has ever cared much for this house. I understand them completely. It seeps into the bones and slows you down. Stay here too long and you will almost certainly lose your edge."

"Indeed," Annika said dryly. "I believe that's called *relaxing*."

And he was not accustomed to acting against

his own self-interest. He could not recall the last time he had wanted something and denied himself.

Only this woman could have inspired such a choice.

He tried to concentrate on that. "You were a virgin, Annika, were you not."

It wasn't a question. And he didn't need an answer. He already knew, but even if he hadn't, he would have gotten the truth from the scalding-hot flush that took over her face. It wouldn't stop there. It would be all over her now, that bright heat sweeping down between her breasts—

She stood taller, as if she wasn't overheating right in front of him. "I feel certain that cannot possibly be relevant to this conversation."

"But you did not tell me, which suggests it was meaningful to you."

"What it was or wasn't hardly matters now."

"You asked me if I could tell." His voice was quiet.

She blanched as if he'd shouted. "You put great stock in *sophistication*, Ranieri. I hated to disappoint. And in any case, you didn't ask me. I didn't think it mattered."

He knew that was not at all what she had thought. And he was beginning to understand exactly why he preferred not to get this close to anyone. Why he preferred to know less, not more, about the women in his life.

This was painful.

Yet he pushed on. "You did not choose to tell me, Annika. It is not the same thing. But it does not matter. I will tell you this. Sex can be powerful. When it's done well, it can feel life altering. You know this now, yes? Yet these are all just feelings. Yours are likely to be more intense, as they are new."

"Wait." She shook her head as if there was too much noise in there for her to concentrate. Or as if he was the noise. "Are you, of all people, lecturing me on *feelings*?"

Ranieri couldn't say he liked the way she asked that. And he liked even less how it landed in him, but he shoved it aside. "I admired your father," he told her, his voice clipped. "I was fond of him. I know that worry over you, and what might become of you, consumed him in those last days before his coma. It pleases me that I've been able to help you on his behalf."

She let out a soft sound that he would not quite call a laugh. "How kind of you. You are known for your kindness, of course." Annika shook her head. "Do you really believe that Bennett Schuyler's dearest wish for his only daughter involved her being sent back home in the middle of her honeymoon?"

He was clenching his jaw and he forced himself to release it. "The fault is mine." At least that part was true. Ranieri inclined his head. "I should have known that making such demands of a virgin might create problems. You don't have the perspective necessary to handle my appetites in full. I should have gone with my first instinct."

And it killed him that as he spoke, she changed. The light in her eyes dimmed. She still clutched her hands before her, but her body—so supple, so soft—had gone rigid.

"I should have gone with mine," she said, and her voice was too cold. Too unlike her. He almost reached out, but he remembered himself in the last moment, and there was nothing to do with her brittle smile but endure it. "I was only sixteen. You came to our front door like a storm cloud and I said to myself, *That man is the devil.* I was right."

"It seems that we were both right," Ranieri gritted out. "All the more reason to stop pretending otherwise, do you not agree?"

And he would never know how long it was they stood there, staring at each other, neither one of them saying a word.

Neither one of them reaching out.

Ranieri told himself this was a good thing. Or if not good, it was the right thing. And that would have to do.

He thought they could have stood there for a lifetime or two, but then the headlights of the car he'd called for her swept through the darkness outside the window, and the spell was broken.

The staff came to get her bags. And she stood there a moment longer, still looking at him with that imploring expression as if she thought that could reach him. As if she was debating whether or not she should throw herself into his arms—

And Ranieri knew that if she did, he would catch her. He wouldn't be able to help himself. But she didn't.

Instead, Annika turned and walked away, and took all the light in the world behind her.

CHAPTER TEN

IT WAS A long and bitter fall.

Back in New York, Annika immersed herself in the life she'd left behind and called herself lucky that it was still there, waiting for her to wake up from the dream she'd been in and remember herself.

Even if she felt a deep well of embarrassment within her because she knew how little she'd wanted to do anything but lose herself in Italy—and in Ranieri—forever.

Well. She liked to call it *embarrassment*, but she knew it was something far deeper than that. It was the way her heart beat now, and the hurt in it. It was the way the world seemed changed all around her. Darker, dimmer. Even in this city that seemed too bright to her after the soft, sultry Italian dark.

When she first landed in New York, she'd almost asked that the car drop her off at her father's old apartment, but bit back the request. Like it or not, she had married Ranieri.

That meant that if he wanted her to move out, he would have to say so and if he did, she would win.

And that was all she had left. Winning this thing.

Ranieri did not come back to New York for three long weeks. And when he did, he was a different man. Or rather, he was the man she'd always thought he was before all of this. Grim. Disapproving. Unimpressed with her in every possible way.

There were no cozy lunches. There were no intimate dinners.

There was no waking up to find him so deep inside her that she was shattering into bright, hot pieces before she'd fully come out of her dreams.

That she cried about these losses, alone in her room at night, was something she would deny if asked. But he never asked. That she had missed him—and still missed him—so horribly that it was like a flu, was something she thought she would rather die than admit.

"Is it already happening?" she asked him one night as they returned from one of the social events he insisted they attend. Because his appearance was always necessary. He left her to handle whatever social niceties were called for and closed business deals over drinks. It would have felt like a partnership, she supposed, if he didn't treat her like a questionable employee. And if she didn't have this regrettable need to torture herself like this, dashing herself against the sullen stone of his new indifference to her. "Are you already cheating on me?"

"I would not consider it cheating if I were," he replied from the other side of the car, his voice sounding gravelly. She glanced at him, watching the lights from the Manhattan street outside the windows wash over his hard face. Harder these days. "You were as blackmailed into this marriage as I was. There was nothing in your father's will about fidelity, Annika. I think you know this."

"Yes or no?"

"And if I say yes?"

It cost her something to shrug then, with such unconcern. Such blasé sophistication. That was what she'd learned, night after night, out swimming with these sharks she liked so little. That was what he wanted, wasn't it?

And it wasn't truly killing her. It only felt like it might.

"Then I will congratulate you and wish you well. The tabloids are certain to make sure the whole world knows if you're cheating, and that would reflect badly on both of us. I was hoping you and I could come to an arrangement before that happens, but not if there's already other women in the mix. That seems entirely too unsavory."

She felt the heat of his gaze on the side of her face. "An arrangement?"

"You're not the only one with needs, Ranieri."

He sighed, managing to make it sound withering. "*Amore*. Please. You are only embarrassing yourself."

She wanted to hurt him then. She actually felt *bloodthirsty*. But she wanted this more. Even if he kept calling her *amore*, which seemed more mocking and pointed each time.

Annika was sure he meant it to feel that way, like a blade beneath her skin. Because he was banking on the possibility that he could win that way.

Because that was the game. Hadn't she thought of it as a game, long ago? And now there was nothing left but to play it.

"I don't feel the slightest bit embarrassed," she told him, still managing to keep her voice cool. "You introduced me to sex. I'd like more of it. If we decide that stepping outside the marriage isn't cheating, then I suppose that opens doors. It just sounds a bit inconvenient, that's all."

And she would never know how she sounded so bored. All the many polished and poisonous society events she'd been forced to attend had finally paid off, apparently. Because she sounded like the rest of them now.

Ranieri let out another one of those sighs. "Forgive me, Annika, but surely what happened in Italy has proven that you cannot handle having sex with me. You become too emotional. You want it to mean things that it cannot."

Yes, she thought balefully. *I am the emotional one here.*

"We live together, I like orgasms, and I thought you could help," she said, impatiently. "But believe me, this conversation makes me wish I was dead. So by all means, find yourself the emotionless mistress of your dreams. I will handle my own needs however I see fit."

He didn't say anything, but when they stepped into his elevator, she was sure she could feel a kind of edgy heat emanating from him. And when the doors opened and let them into his apartment, she'd taken all of three angry strides when he was on her.

And it wasn't like Italy. It wasn't languorous. It wasn't an endless, rolling delight, or feeling as if the two of them were one.

It was hot. Furious. He lifted her up, dug beneath her dress, and dragged her legs around his waist. Then he held her there, pressing her back against the nearest wall, as he reached between them to free himself, ripped off her panties, then plunged deep.

It was a mad gallop to a blistering finish, and when he was done, when she was limp and wheezing, he stepped back and fixed himself while she clung to the wall and pretended she really believed her legs could hold her.

"Sleep well, *amore*," he said, his voice dark, then he left her there.

And for some time in those darkest days of the year, that was what it was like between them. They lived separate lives. They came together for the usual social events. And there was sex, but it was always about the goal, not the journey.

There was nothing wrong with that, necessarily. It was still mind-blowing. It was still Ranieri.

But she knew the shift was deliberate.

And, yes, when it was done she would sob out her love, her loneliness into her shower, but surely as long as no one knew that but her it didn't count. It swirled its way down the drain and was gone again by morning.

Annika just kept telling herself that she could live with it. One way or another, she *would* live with it.

Not because you want to win this, that voice would whisper as she lay in her bed, alone, her eyes swollen from tears. *But because you cannot bear to leave him, even now.*

It was obvious to her that she'd missed something that day with his parents. Not everybody was lucky enough to have family they admired, the way she had admired and loved her father, and the memories of her mother. Not everyone had even a family they liked. If anything, meeting Ranieri's parents had made her love who he'd made himself even more.

Because they'd certainly given him no guidance. In anything. That much was clear.

She knew that he'd decided to end what had been happening between the two of them because of that day even though she'd thought they'd handled the situation about as well as it could have been handled.

The real truth, that she could admit only late, late at night when her heart ached for him, was that Annika persisted in believing that if she could just hold on, he would come back to her.

But as the long, cold fall wore on, Ranieri showed no signs of blinking.

It was coming on the middle of December when she caught up with one of her college friends one evening. It was a chilly night, though outside, the city was festive. She had become adept at avoiding the paparazzi these days, or perhaps they'd finally grown bored with her. Either way, she had no photographers on her tail when she slipped into a quiet booth in the sort of restaurant Ranieri would never frequent, looking forward to an evening of nostalgia and laughter in thankfully unpretentious surroundings.

But her friend was looking at her mobile phone

when Annika sat down, and smiled oddly when she looked up again. "Congratulations, Annika. It looks like you won."

"I won?" Annika shook her head, not understanding. "What did I win?"

Her friend swiveled the screen of her phone around and showed it to Annika. "It says it right here. Ranieri Furlan is leaving the Schuyler Corporation. Annika. *You did it*."

And later, her friend would tell her that it was as if Annika had been hit in the head. She had stared back at that phone for far too long. She didn't respond when her friend tried to speak to her.

Then she'd simply stood and walked out.

Annika wasn't aware of any of that. She had a vague impression of running down a side street on the Upper West Side, then angrily hailing a taxi out on Columbus. Then she sat in the back of the cab and stared out blankly at storefronts and bodegas done up in holiday splendor, crowds on the street, and the usual outraged honking from too many vehicles trying to make their way around Manhattan.

She suffered through the slowest elevator in the history of the universe at Ranieri's loft down in Tribeca, but when it finally opened on his floor, he wasn't home. She even checked up on the roof, though she knew he rarely ventured there.

But he was nowhere to be found, so she headed

to the only other place she knew he was likely to be, even in the wake of his announcement.

And just like the last time she'd marched into the Schuyler Corporation offices bearing a potted plant, the reception desk was no match for her.

"You can't just walk back there," the poor woman tried to tell her.

Annika smiled. "Do you know who I am?" she asked. Nicely, she thought.

Wide-eyed, the woman nodded.

"Wonderful, then you know my name."

"Yes, Mrs. Furlan." The woman bit the name off, not that Annika could blame her. "I know who you are and your name, but—"

"That's Annika *Schuyler* Furlan," Annika corrected her, jabbing her finger toward the logo on the wall behind the woman's head. "That's my name right there. I think I can go where I want, don't you?"

She didn't get the impression the woman did think that. But Annika knew she wouldn't stop her. And it felt like déjà vu to march down these halls again, this time unencumbered by a pot of dahlias. But weighed down all the same, this time by what she wished was a righteous fury—but she was fairly certain it was fear.

Just sheer terror that he was really leaving the company, and therefore her.

He wasn't in his office, so she turned and marched along the same hall he'd once escorted her down with his arm around her shoulders. And that silly plant held before him.

And it felt not only right, but good to throw open the doors of his conference room and march in once again.

This time, Ranieri was the only one inside. He sat at the head of the table, surrounded by what appeared to be even more stacks of paper, file folders, and not one but two laptops.

"Hello, Annika," he said, with only a brief glance up her way. He managed to make that withering, too. "I take it you've heard the news."

She only realized now that she'd been running around this whole time—through the city, through his loft, through this office—because it was difficult to catch her breath. But she made herself slow down and try, because she could tell by the way he was deliberately not looking at her that he was trying to get under her skin. He expected her to fly off the handle.

And she understood that though this felt like one more round of their same game, the stakes tonight were higher.

The stakes tonight were everything.

As if he hadn't already conceded.

Oddly enough, that made her think she still had a chance to change his mind.

And she had been waiting all this time for just this. Just one chance.

"I went into your office before I came here," she said, a strange sort of calm washing through her despite the hurry and rush and worry that had propelled her here. She studied him. "I see you still have our plant. The embodiment of our love."

He threw his pen onto the pad before him and sat back in his chair, then took a moment to make a meal out of arranging his features into something suggesting an attempt at patience more than patience itself. "I cannot claim to have a green thumb, of course. That would be my assistant. Gregory can make anything grow, apparently."

Even your silly plant, was the obvious next line, though he didn't say it.

"I only have one question for you," Annika said, instead of chasing down the things he hadn't said.

And she wished that she'd known what this night would bring. She would have dressed the way he liked best. That sophistication, that hint of glamour. Because he'd taught her the language of fine clothing and she was fluent in it now. Instead, she'd spent the day in the museum and had dressed for that, followed by a dinner with an old college friend. She was wearing her usual uniform of jeans tucked into boots and a cozy sweater to keep the chill off. But if she was right—and she had to be right, or she didn't know what she would do with herself, or how she would possibly survive this—none of that actually mattered.

She moved farther into the room, peeling off her coat and tossing it on the conference room table. Then she kept going until she could take the seat catty-corner to him, pulling it in close so she was right there. Right next to him.

Then it was her turn to put on a little show of resting her chin on her hands and gazing at him as if her whole life hung in the balance here.

Because it did.

"Whatever you're about to do or say, don't," Ranieri said, his voice forbidding. Not so much withering as gruff. "No round of rainbow unicorns is going to change anything. There is nothing that requires changing, in any case. I have simply come to the conclusion that the inconvenience of looking for another company to run pales in comparison to the inconvenience of being married."

"You don't actually mean *married*, though," Annika corrected him, and though it was a fight to keep her voice even, she managed it. "You mean married to *me*. Because you take your grandfather's position on this one, don't you? You should be allowed to do whatever you want, without question. Isn't that right?"

His eyes blazed, and that stark mouth of his thinned.

"Yes," he said, though his jaw looked tight enough to shatter. "Precisely."

She could have pointed out how little he thought of his grandfather's pride, but she didn't. She could have asked him if he thought that his own father's behavior, not to mention his marriage, perhaps followed on directly from the choices his grandfather had made. It seemed like a straight line to her. But she didn't ask him that, either.

Because all of that was noise.

Last night had been a rare night without an event, so she'd gone up to the roof to sit in the hot tub for a while. Then she'd stood out in the cold until it made her shake before going into the hot water again.

She called it therapy.

When she'd come back down into the loft, Ranieri had been finishing a call. He'd tossed his cell phone aside as he came in the kitchen. One look at her, her hair piled on top of her head, wearing nothing but a robe, his golden eyes had gone molten.

And the next thing she'd known, Annika had been flat on her back in his bed and he had been pounding into her in another scalding, blistering rush to that beautiful finish.

But when she'd made as if to roll away, to gather her robe and make her way back to her room—lest she get any ideas that might turn into emotions, the horror—he had pulled her back into place beside him.

He had taken her again and again that night.

The last time, so late at night it had become early the next morning, it had been like that final morning in Italy.

Slow. Intense.

Shattering, inside and out.

When she'd woken up hours later to find herself still in his bed, he'd been gone.

But she understood now.

She reached over and gripped his hands in hers, holding tight because she expected him to pull away.

"Ranieri." Annika said his name softly, like some kind of prayer. "When did you decide that you were doomed, no matter what you did?"

CHAPTER ELEVEN

Her words went through him like a thunderclap.

Ranieri jerked back, and only some distant hint of self-preservation kept him from leaping out of his chair and doing something he would never have forgiven himself for—like plastering himself to the far wall.

As if he was some kind of excitable feline.

His heart careened about inside his chest anyway. Surely he didn't have to *show* it.

He regarded her for a long, tense moment.

"I don't know what you mean," he gritted out.

But Annika didn't look as if she was trying to fight with him. It was far worse than that. She looked…compassionate.

It was unbearable.

"This is exactly what I was afraid of," he seethed at her. "This indiscriminate emotion just flung about. This is a conference room. We are in an office building. This is no place—"

"I love you," Annika said, and could not have silenced him in any more effective manner. And then she made it worse by smiling. "Though I think you know that. Or you wouldn't be reacting this way."

This time, Ranieri did push back from the table. He stood, though he still did not cling to the wall. He stalked to the bank of windows and tried to orient himself in the ever-shifting, ever-changing city at his feet.

Manhattan seemed infinitely easier to take on than the woman behind him.

The woman he couldn't seem to escape—even when she wasn't in the same room. She had haunted him across the planet. Even now, he was sure he could catch the hint of her scent in the air, that perfect vanilla, yet better.

Much better.

"But it's even worse than that, isn't it?" she asked from behind him. "It's far worse."

And how could he have guessed, all those years ago, that this woman would be the end of him? That the daughter of a business associate he had only ever noticed to criticize could wreck him so easily?

Because he knew what she was going to say. Every muscle in his body tensed.

"You love me, too, Ranieri."

He turned back around to face her then, everything inside him a frenzy of heat and need and feeling and *her*.

"And what a gift that will be for you," he all but snarled at her. "The love of a Furlan. Where would you like to isolate yourself, *amore*? Tell me, where do you think you would most like to hide away your broken heart while I betray you again and again and again? Because I will. We always do."

"I'm not your grandmother," she replied.

She stood up from the table then, coming around the end of it and heading straight for him.

Ranieri could not imagine how he had ever thought that this woman was plain. That she was anything but what he saw before him now.

Fierce and glorious with it. Carelessly sophisticated.

So beautiful it hurt.

That was the trouble. That was what he couldn't seem to get around. This woman *hurt* him. He looked at her and he hurt. He touched her and he hurt.

He had built himself an entire life to avoid hurt. He had walled himself off in a fortress of money and power. And none of that had mattered at all.

Annika Schuyler had walked right past his defenses and insinuated herself so deep inside him that now when he was without her, that hurt, too.

Ranieri didn't know what to *do* about her—and that was a new sensation for him. He always knew what to do.

"Not only am I not your grandmother," she was saying as she came toward him, "you'll notice that I haven't given you any ultimatums. I haven't asked you to give up anything at all. That must be very frustrating for you, Ranieri. Because that was clearly your brilliant plan."

He made a low noise, something too close to a growl. "I don't understand how you could put up with a husband who treats you as I do. What does that say about you?"

But she laughed. That silky brown hair spilled all around her, and she laughed.

"It says that I'm in love with an idiot," she replied, still coming closer to him, so that he had to worry that he might not keep his hands to himself. That he might give in to that fire in him all over again. "And I've been waiting him out."

He wanted to order her to keep her distance, but he couldn't do it.

And he had brought this upon himself. He should never have allowed her to convince him that they should bring sex back into their marriage. He'd known better.

But the truth was, he had spent three gruesome

weeks alone in Shanghai and had been weak with longing. Weak for her.

Always and only for her.

And at first, Ranieri had been confident he could keep himself under control. Treating sex between them like it was no more than scratching an itch couldn't last. He'd expected that she would object. It would be too much for her. He was certain she would break down one of these nights and demand more. Demand better.

But he'd been the one who'd broken last night. He'd happened upon her in the kitchen, rosy from the hot tub's heat, wrapped in nothing but a soft robe, like a fantasy he hadn't known he'd had. He had kept her in his bed, making love to her again and again. Until this morning, when he'd realized there was no part of him that wanted to leave her in that bed.

There was no part of him that wanted to leave her at all.

That was when he'd understood, in the starkest possible terms, the magnitude of his mistake.

There had only been one possible thing left to do. Only one out, and he'd taken it. And had then spent the day in crisis talks with the Schuyler Corporation's Board of Directors.

And yet the only thing he could seem to think about was Annika.

Who'd been waiting him out all this time.

"I love you, Ranieri," she said again, her voice that much fiercer now that she was closer. Her green eyes ablaze.

And she didn't stop when she reached him. She kept right on going until she rested her palms on his chest.

He reached up to pull her hands away from him, because touching led nowhere manageable. He'd tried that. But he found himself holding her hands instead. Cradled in his, as if this was a proposal instead of him ending what should never have been started.

Not that Annika seemed to be getting the message.

"I think I've loved you as long as I've known you," she told him, her words seeming to collide with all the places he *hurt* inside. "It's not an accident that you're the only man I've been with. You *are* the only man, Ranieri. The only man I ever thought about in all my life, so how could it ever have been anyone but you?"

And even now, when he should know better, there was that current of deep male satisfaction deep inside him. Because he couldn't help liking that she thought such things.

But surely that proved that he was exactly who

he thought he was. Just another Furlan. Full of himself and unworthy of anyone else's love and regard.

Fear and awe in the corporate world had sustained him this long. Surely he should need nothing more.

"You deserve far better than me," he managed to grit out.

"And you deserve to believe that you are capable of loving another person without destroying them," she said, her voice intense, her green eyes steady. "Because Ranieri. Listen to me. *You are*."

He felt something move through him, like a deep shudder. As if he was breaking into pieces when he knew he wasn't. Because she was holding him—with that gaze, with her hands in his.

She was holding him, and because of that, he was whole.

Even when he didn't feel as if he ought to have been.

"You visited my father every single day you were in this city," Annika continued, her voice low and fierce. "He was in a coma. There was no possible advantage to be gained from visiting him. No corporate reason that would explain it. I suspect you loved him. Because you went and sat with him. Every day you could, Ranieri. For five years."

He had done that. And had explained it away a

thousand different times. He'd spoken of respect. Of proper behavior.

He would never have called it love. He had no experience with love, in any case.

But now, looking back, he couldn't think what else it could have been.

Because now he knew what love was.

Annika had showed him.

"You could have laughed off those additions to my father's will," she said. "So could I. Yes, I love Schuyler House, but there were other ways I could have gone about taking charge of it. But we jumped right into this marriage instead."

"Passion fades, Annika," he said, urgently now. "And then what are you left with?"

But she only shook her head at him. "Passion fades not because passion itself is temporary. But because it can't be the only thing that links two people together. If it is, then of course, in time, it will fade. But what if it's sustained by other things? Love? Respect? Genuine affection? Why would that fade?"

He moved without meaning to, freeing one hand so he could gently cup her face. "Because you're the expert on these things."

Her gaze lightened then, but she didn't smile. "I'm an expert on you, Ranieri. I've studied you for years. Falling in love with you was a slow process that took most of my life, and then a whirlwind these few months. But it was always inevitable."

"Annika. *Amore*," he managed to say. "I cannot bear the idea that one day, without even meaning to, you and I will become my parents."

"That will never happen," she assured him, with another flash of that ferocity he loved to see in her. "Because you are not a small man, forever looking to others to make you large. And I am not a dissatisfied woman, looking for others to blame." Her lips curved then. At last. "And I always know that if all else fails, I can always roll out the unicorn initiative and get you right where I want you."

Ranieri shocked himself by laughing. Because that was what she did to him.

And suddenly, he got it. In a way he never had before. This whole time, he'd reeled from one emotion to the next, convinced that being with her was fracturing. That she was breaking him down into all these pieces—and he could only assume that this was how it began. Losing his sense of who he was, and then, and inexorably, turning into all the things he liked least about his family.

But now he knew better.

The trouble with his family was that they felt nothing. They thought only of themselves. But with Annika, he felt everything.

Everything.

He had thought of little but her since the day of that will reading. If not long before, during his five years of acting as some kind of guardian to her.

And loving her, with everything he was, with all these different parts, was the only way he would ever be anything like whole.

"Annika," he managed to say, because he got it now, and he was filled and whole and new, "I love you."

Her smile then was so brilliant, so bright, it drowned out the city outside.

"I know," she whispered. "I know you do. I love you, too."

Ranieri only remembered at the last moment that he was in the conference room in the middle of the Schuyler Corporation offices. The walls were made almost entirely of glass and half the company was right on the other side, no doubt watching every moment of this.

It would be the very opposite of appropriate to handle this moment the way he wanted to, naked and horizontal.

So he did the next best thing.

Fully aware that he would likely see a video of what he was about to do on the nightly news, Ranieri Furlan swallowed back the damnable pride that had done nothing for him in all his life, and dropped down to his knees.

"You have already married me," he said, gazing up at her as her gaze widened. "But Annika, I want you to be my wife. In full. No restrictions, no rules. I want to build a life with you and I want it all. All those words we said in our vows, I want to make them real. Sickness. Health. Richer and poor. I want them all. And I want you by my side, always."

She looked down at him, her eyes sparkling, that fathomless green. "Where else would I be?"

"I want to love you as well out of bed as I do in it," he told her gruffly, not sure he could even put into words these things he felt. But he could try. "And I promise you, I will not let the Furlan pride tear us apart. I vow it with all that I am."

"Oh," she said, though she was smiling big and bright, "you don't have to worry about that."

He gripped her hands. "Since that day in the law firm, when I heard your father's wishes, I have worried about little else."

But she smiled down at him. His wife. His love. His future.

And her smile was beautiful, as it always was, but there was steel in her gaze.

"I have my own pride," she told him then, very matter-of-factly. "And I do not intend to let you go, or to suffer in silence in some cottage in the hills, no matter how beautiful it is. If we're going to do this, Ranieri, then we do it together. All the way. Or not at all."

"That sounds like an ultimatum."

But he was smiling up at her, and she could have given him a thousand ultimatums then, for all he cared. He would have met each one.

"It's only an ultimatum if you think it's a choice," she replied, grinning. "I'm speaking of facts. That's the way it's going to be with us. I'm going to make sure of it."

"And I am going to hold you to it, Annika. Every day. For the rest of our lives."

She leaned down to kiss him, sweet and hot, and when she pulled back, they were both grinning wide. Because this was how it was going to be.

This was the beginning of the beautiful life they would build—together, this time.

Ranieri knew it. He had already created fortunes out of thin air. He defied expectations as a matter of course. He had somehow won the love of this woman when he knew he could never deserve it, or her—though he intended to dedicate his life to the art of trying.

Forever would be a piece of cake in comparison.

He would make sure of it.

CHAPTER TWELVE

ON THE FIRST anniversary of their wedding, Ranieri presented his wife with a dahlia in a pot, this time a deep shade of purple.

She only smiled, then gave him his present.

A rainbow unicorn figurine, of course. This one the size of a football.

He placed it on his desk in his office and dared anyone who saw it to comment, but they never did. No one dared.

The Schuyler Corporation had come to the conclusion that his announcement that he was leaving was a bid for better compensation, and Ranieri had felt so guilty about that that he'd donated the difference to charity—and upped the rest of his charitable contributions by double-digit percentage points.

Because at this point, he couldn't lose his fortune if he tried. So he figured he might as well try harder.

He and Annika carried on together, exactly as

planned. Only with more laughter than he could have imagined. More love, more light.

That was their life together. *More.*

And on their second wedding anniversary, she presented him with a daughter.

They moved out of his Tribeca loft with the daughter who had been lovingly created in the rooftop bathhouse, back into the Schuyler Apartments on Fifth Avenue.

Where they had three floors, after all.

It was no wonder they did their best to fill them.

Ten years later, Ranieri stood in the sitting room outside their bedroom in the house in the Italian hills, where it was their custom to spend the summer far away from the demands of his job, and hers. Far away from city life and the distractions of too much technology.

He heard Annika coming, calling out as she went, corralling the children and issuing her usual commands.

When she arrived in the sitting room, she looked flushed and disheveled and more beautiful today than she had been all those years ago. She smiled when she saw him, the way she always did, and handed him the baby she held on her hip.

Their final baby, they had decided. After three girls, all of them stunners like their mother. And three boys, all of them impossible, Annika liked to say, just like him. This last had been their tiebreaker.

Accordingly, he was the most mischievous of the lot.

Ranieri loved him, as he loved all of them, with a love so deep it bordered on grief—and he had learned how to live with that.

"Are you all right?" Annika asked him now.

He followed her into their bedroom, watching as she bustled around. He found he loved this season of their lives, where the passion he always felt for her only grew—but he was always having to wait. Until the children were in bed. Until they had a moment alone. Until she took that nap she would pretend she didn't need, but always made her feel refreshed.

But Ranieri had discovered something he never would have known without her. That delayed gratification only made it better.

"I am all right," he assured her. "In every possible way."

Annika threw him a look, but she didn't comment further. Then again, she didn't have to. The longer they stayed together, the more they simply knew each other. Better and better by the day.

He couldn't wait to see what that looked like twenty years from now. Thirty.

And perhaps later, when they were alone in their bed and the children were safely tucked away in theirs, he would tell her what it was like to see his parents again as they had today. To see them the way he did these days. To feel nothing but pity.

He had vowed to Annika in a conference room in New York that he would love her forever, and he would. He did.

But what he never could have guessed—what seeing his diminished parents only made clear—was that love, deep and sure and not afraid of what life might throw at them, with vulnerability in place of pride, was pure joy.

She came past him on one of her bustling loops, and he stopped her with his free arm, pulling her face to his to kiss her, deep and long, while their baby chortled with delight.

When he pulled away, her eyes were dreamy and still that glorious green. And her smile made him start imagining all the things he planned to do to her later. In detail.

"What was that for?" she asked softly.

"For you," he said. He kissed her again. And only pulled back when the baby started squawking. "Always for you, *mi amore*. Light of my life, I cannot thank you enough."

"You never need to thank me," she whispered. "You don't need to do anything but love me, Ranieri. Always."

"I will," he promised her, the way he did at least twice a day. "Forever."

And then, after they put all their babies to bed, he stretched out with her in that bed in the back of the house that they had made a home, not a hiding place, and he showed her.

Again and again, because forever took the best kind of work.

And he was just the man for the job.

* * * * *

If you were blown away by
Willed to Wed Him
then be sure to catch up on
Crowning His Lost Princess
and
Reclaiming His Ruined Princess
Caitlin Crews's thrilling
The Lost Princess Scandal duet!

Also why not dive into these other stories
by Caitlin Crews?

Her Deal with the Greek Devil
The Sicilian's Forgotten Wife
The Bride He Stole for Christmas
The Scandal That Made Her His Queen

Available now!

#4041 THE KING'S CHRISTMAS HEIR
The Stefanos Legacy
by Lynne Graham
When Lara rescued Gaetano from a blizzard, she never imagined she'd say "I do" to the man with no memory. Or, when the revelation that he's actually a future king rips their passionate marriage apart, that she'd be expecting a precious secret!

#4042 CINDERELLA'S SECRET BABY
Four Weddings and a Baby
by Dani Collins
Innocent Amelia's encounter with Hunter was unforgettable... and had life-changing consequences! After learning Hunter was engaged, she vowed to raise their daughter alone. But now, Amelia's secret is suddenly, scandalously exposed!

#4043 CLAIMED BY HER GREEK BOSS
by Kim Lawrence
Playboy CEO Ezio will do anything to save the deal of a lifetime. Even persuade his prim personal assistant, Matilda, to take a six-month assignment in Greece...as his convenient bride!

#4044 PREGNANT INNOCENT BEHIND THE VEIL
Scandalous Royal Weddings
by Michelle Smart
Her whole life, Princess Alessia has put the royal family first, until the night she let her desire for Gabriel reign supreme. Now she's pregnant! And to avoid a scandal, that duty demands a hasty royal wedding...

HPCNMRA0822

#4045 THEIR DESERT NIGHT OF SCANDAL
Brothers of the Desert
by Maya Blake

Twenty-four hours in the desert with Sheikh Tahir is more than Lauren bargained for when she came to ask for his help. Yet their inescapable intimacy empowers Lauren to lay bare the scandalous truth of their shared past—and her still-burning desire for Tahir...

#4046 AWAKENED BY THE WILD BILLIONAIRE
by Bella Mason

Colliding with a masked stranger at a ball sends shy Emma's pulse skyrocketing. And that's *before* he introduces himself as Alexander Hastings, the CEO with a wild side, which puts him way out of her league! Will Emma step out of the shadows and into the billionaire's penthouse?

#4047 THE MARRIAGE THAT MADE HER QUEEN
Behind the Palace Doors...
by Kali Anthony

To claim her crown, queen-to-be Lise must wed. The man she must turn to is Rafe, the self-made billionaire who once made her believe in love. He'll have to make her believe in it again for passion to be part of their future...

#4048 STRANDED WITH HIS RUNAWAY BRIDE
by Julieanne Howells

Surrendering her power to a man is unacceptable to Princess Violetta. Even *if* that man sets her alight with a single glance! But when Prince Leo tracks his runaway bride down and they are stranded together, he's not the enemy she first thought...

YOU CAN FIND MORE INFORMATION ON UPCOMING HARLEQUIN TITLES, FREE EXCERPTS AND MORE AT HARLEQUIN.COM.

HPCNMRB0822

*Colliding with a masked stranger at a ball sends
shy Emma's pulse skyrocketing. And that's before he
introduces himself as Alexander Hastings,
the CEO with a wild side, which puts him
way out of her league! Will Emma step out of the
shadows and into the billionaire's penthouse?*

*Read on for a sneak preview of Bella Mason's
debut story for Harlequin Presents,*
Awakened by the Wild Billionaire.

"Emma," Alex said, pinning her against the wall in a spectacularly graffitied alley, the walls an ever-changing work of art, when he could bear it no more. "I have to tell you. I really don't care about seeing the city. I just want to get you back in my bed."

He could barely believe that he wanted to take her back home. Sending her on her way was the smarter plan. But how smart was it really to deny himself? Emma knew the score. This wasn't about feelings or a relationship. It was just sex.

"Give me the weekend. I promise you won't regret it." His voice was low and rough. He could see in her eyes that she knew just how aroused he was, and with his body against hers, she could feel it.

"I want that too," she breathed.

"What I said before still stands. This doesn't change things."

"I know that." She grinned. "I don't want it to."

Don't miss
Awakened by the Wild Billionaire
available October 2022 wherever
Harlequin Presents books and ebooks are sold.

Harlequin.com

HPEXP0822